DIG
ST

'An outstanding collection - as rich, diverse and surprising as the district to which it is dedicated.'
JONATHAN COE, multi-award winning author

'What a lively, inventive gifted diversity of stories! Who'd have thought that Digbeth – that ever changing, never resting square-mile – could express so much about our much-loved unpretentious city? Or that it could so readily provide such talent and such artistry.'
JIM CRACE, Whitbread Novel award winning author

'A raw and characterful collection that is both a reflection and tribute to the greatness of Digbeth, and to the resilience and indefatigability of small independent publishers.'
TARIQ GODDARD, author and publisher, Repeater Books

'They say that Digbeth is where Birmingham began, the location of the first settlement. That Digbeth came first is typical of the place. It is a centre of innovation and change, a hub of creativity, and now the source of some unique writing. I hope readers will enjoy these brand new Digbeth voices.'
STEVEN KNIGHT, writer/creator, *Peaky Blinders*

'A fiery depiction of an inner-city village across the decades. A fitting reminder of the second city's burgeoning talent pool.'
JENNY LECOAT, New York Times bestselling author

'Filled with snippets of life in all its frank and poignant beauty, this is a great read for anyone, and a must for those with a connection to Birmingham.'
ELIZABETH LEE, author, *Cunning Women*

'The writing is a pitch-perfect reflection of a city rich in diversity, energy and untold story. Digbeth Stories is a powerful collection of work which shines light on the creativity of our self-effacing second city.'
NATALIE MARLOW, author, *Needless Alley*

Slip between worlds, wander alleyways and cut-throughs, explore the wormholes that exist between the red bricked Victorian gothic and the spray canned arty heart of the city. Here is urban glory. A truly great and gritty read.
EMMA PURSHOUSE, writer and performance poet

DIGBETH STORIES

Edited by

GARRIE FLETCHER

PETER HAYNES

NIGEL PROCTOR

FLOODGATE

First Floodgate paperback edition July 2023

www.floodgatepress.co.uk

A catalogue record for this book is available from the British Library.

Paperback ISBN: 978-1-7394395-0-7

Digbeth Stories is typeset in Baskerville Neo and Monotype Clarendon.

John Baskerville (1707–1775) Born in Wolverley. Made in Birmingham.

Cover design by Tor © Floodgate

Typeset by Peter Burgess

Printed by ImprintDigital.com

Contents

Introduction

PETER HAYNES

Take a walk through Digbeth today and you might see one of many things: a post-industrial ruin; a network of mouldering canals; a building site for HS2; a burgeoning and bohemian centre for start-ups and pop-ups and theme bars and street art. You might see new builds, and very old builds only held together by buddleia and hope. You might see streets named after long-buried freshwater springs that provided fertile ground for growth through Digbeth's long history. That growth brought manufacturing, trade, construction, and craft. And it brought people from all over the world.

Today the city and its conurbation comprise a million inhabitants – not bad for a place that was a minor presence on the map a few hundred years ago. The city welcomed all people regardless of background so long as they could make, build, *sweat* for the place.

Who were those people? Who are its people now?

Read on to find out.

We think Birmingham, and Digbeth in particular, is something interesting to write about. So do the contributors to this collection.

And it feels right that we do it now.

Digbeth is in the midst of a transformation (the same could be said for the whole city, constantly recycling itself and half-resembling a building site most days), thanks in a large part to the knock-it-down-and-start-over actors from the High Speed Rail 2 contingent. It's already changed since we kicked off this project, and thus it will ever be. Part of the reason we wanted to do this was to capture a sense of the place as it was and still is, before it's levelled and that sense of the place changes from *bold, broken,* and *boutique* to merely *big brands*.

Why else did we do this? Well, it's time some new writing from Birmingham was seen and read. The city is guilty of hiding its light – a side effect of its work-a-day humble origins – but there are people who believe it is a place to be seen, felt, tasted, *experienced*. When we put out the call for new writing about the city, we weren't sure we'd get any submissions at all, but we were wrong. The writing was out there, and it came in all forms, reflecting the concerns and fascinations of the city itself.

So, what do we have in this collection? In brief, a right mixed bag. Here we see everything from Digbeth's deep past right up to the present day. We have real life flâneurials, social commentary and wry observation. We have fictional takes on the city from the realistic to the speculative. We have ghosts, glamour, and celebrations. There's something for everyone.

Digbeth has strong bones. It has been said that without Digbeth there would be no Birmingham. Many cities have a district like Digbeth – the birthplace of major industries that shouldered a whole city and generated the fire and smoke in its belly – but there's nowhere quite like our Digbeth. The industry has mostly gone now, but the stories remain. We hope you enjoy reading it as much as we enjoyed making it.

We are indebted to many people for helping us
put this together, not least of which are
Kit de Waal and Jonathan Davidson
of Writing West Midlands,
both proud flag-bearers for the Brum creative scene.

And to Helena Bacon, our copy editor.
This collection benefits enormously
from her clear-sighted light touch.

THE EDITORS

River Rea

RACHEL SAMBROOKS

It's six o clock in the morning, just me and the River Rea passing by, speaking in riddles.

They had a raid two doors down, woke me up and I didn't want to say nothing but we seen him moving out yesterday. He left the equipment in the loft they said. Took the plants with him.

Three a.m. bloody sirens going. I'm walking me dogs at six on no sleep. Millie's taking her time cos she's on her last legs but the vet says she's too fat so I got to walk her.

There's me and the dogs wading through the sea of flood on the fields scaring off the seagulls. It's just broken over the grass at the back not in the streets like before. They reckon it was the builders up the hill damming up their end and making us have the run-off because they don't want their muck in their own place.

Not in the posh houses do they.

Giving us all their run-off.

Now would you look at that. Who's done that? Bloody leaving chip packets on the floor for me to pick up. Can't reach that one stuck on the bank in the broken weeds. Nothing better to do, have they?

When the river burst her banks the widow up the road lost everything and she didn't have insurance or nothing.

Them kids next door travelled off to France in a van.

Anyway, I don't mind, we're alright. Got the sandbags out.

You want to see them sitting on our front wall puffing away but what else they got? One boy, he looks forty and he's a teenager come from that shelter in the corner. Now he's wandering up past me on the way to wait for the man to come home. He isn't coming home, bab, alright, they picked him up at three.

These streets were for workers, then it was full of students, squeeze twenty into a house for four, now they're all doss houses. Selling on, buying up, renting out, each house rebuilt and dried out – recycling the floodwater.

But it's not a flood, it's revenge.

Any minute now, the Rea, she'll hit Digbeth and get buried underground. Go invisible in the culvert between the bricks.

She runs straight past ours and sometimes bursts out in a rage at the back, demanding we notice she's there.

I greet the river as we walk past, dogs toddling after, the deep wide sky. It's paradise and she wants to stay here sometimes. Doesn't want to get buried and labelled into nothingness under the weight of the city.

There's a street of buried people here. Like him off with his mental things and hers got two kids by herself and some of us are too old to learn how to work an expresso machine. They want us to be working but we used to be always making things like pearl buttons or specs, glass eyes or lardy cakes and there's nothing to make now except coffee and phone calls.

The river's seen it all. She's fleeing the scene of the crime, hiding behind walls and pretending she's a dribble of a stream or a canal. Waiting for her chance to strike.

Berkhead

KATE MASCARENHAS

Kim Burke feels guilty about a lot of things she did in her teens. Here is just one.

It was March 1986. At that time Kim lived with her brother Eugene, and their mom, on the top floor of Gooch House, a four-storey block of flats. Today Eugene is a computer operator who walks with a limp. In March 1986, he was nearly eight. He was obsessed with his BMX. On the morning Kim built the bridge, he woke at dawn — as he did every day — and rode his bicycle from the flat into the lift. He waited until he reached the ground floor; then he rode out again, past Mr. Fitzpatrick's, past the boarded-up bike shed, and into the play area. There was a round climbing frame meant for toddlers. It stood only a couple of feet high. The bars were just wide enough to accommodate Eugene's wheels. He liked to circle the edge for four or five hours at a time. The previous week, Mr. Fitzpatrick had grasped him round the ribcage and pulled Eugene away because he wouldn't get off when he was told. Eugene went rigid with rage, then screamed and bit Mr. Fitzpatrick on the forearm. He didn't break the flesh through Fitzpatrick's shirt. But he left a crescent of bruises, each the size of a milk tooth.

Their mother said Eugene was *wilful*. Sometimes Kim wondered if Eugene wasn't so much wilful as taking the piss. In all weathers he insisted on wearing his blue anorak, which had a tangerine lining and fake fur trim. He always let the sleeves slide down to his elbows. Their mom used to nag that he'd overheat himself, until he escaped from the flat wearing his anorak and nothing else. She went out to hang the washing on the balcony, and saw him cycling in the car park below, with only a strip of nylon for modesty.

Kim tried to ignore him. This was hard for two reasons. First, the other kids thought he was weird. They called him BMX Berk, and sang songs about him riding his bike in the nude. Not that he cared. Second, he shared her room. She was older than him by five years. Before he started school they had been close. Each night she would tell him stories in the dark, and pass him squares of Caramac chocolate, which was his favourite. He liked stories about the canals. Once, when Kim was very small, their mom had walked her through one of the canal tunnels and stared at the mural painted on the curved wall, tapping it with a chipped fingernail. *That's your father, Pinket Jack*, she'd said, naming the man in the picture. He carried a basket of gold and coral and shifted between worlds. He could talk with animals. So Kim made up stories about him, and passed them on.

But now Kim was thirteen Eugene still wanted to play games she was too old for. She wished he'd grow up. There were kids in every flat on the fourth floor. You couldn't escape if they thought you were a joke. But lately Kim thought she had a chance of getting in with Lisa down the hall, who wore a bra and nicked lipsticks from Boots. Not that Lisa needed to nick anything. Kim's mom said Lisa was spoilt. All the same Kim let herself be talked into pinching a packet of roll caps. They intended to fire them from the balcony. There wasn't the chance, though; Kim's mom found them in the sock drawer. She didn't hold with toy guns. Eugene said he had stolen them. This only furthered Kim's exasperation. She was tired of hurtling from embarrassment to loyalty and back.

On Saint Patrick's day, the city's people gathered to see a procession of garlanded floats. The streets of Digbeth smelt of stout. Several children strayed from the parade, leaving their parents in the pubs and at the roadside. Music followed the children as they meandered back to Gooch House. Lisa, Anthony, Christian, Marcus, Amanda and, slightly apart from the others, Kim. On the corner of Gooch House, an overfull skip caught their attention.

Amanda, the littlest of them, scratched her left calf with her right toe. She wore yellow jelly sandals with ankle socks.

'What's so good about a skip?' she asked.

Lisa evidently thought skips were fascinating. She hoisted herself up the side and picked her way over the debris. The crags of plaster and brick made an impressive platform. Kim noticed Lisa was wearing shorts. What was it her mom said? *Legs all the way up to her knickers.*

A few kids from the fourth floor sat on the kerb, watching.

'Lookit all this wood,' Lisa said. There were a dozen floorboards which she was tossing out on to the tarmac one by one. Marcus from flat 24 ducked a stray nail.

'These are dead straight,' Kim said, kneeling to see. 'We could put'um on the staircase and skate down.'

To Kim's satisfaction, Lisa looked at her approvingly.

'Nah,' said Anthony, from flat 19. 'We'd get bollocked by Fitzpatrick if he heard us on the stairs.'

Lisa glanced at Fitzpatrick's window. Then her eyes wandered, with more interest, to the balcony above.

She smiled.

'I got another idea.'

She pointed.

'See them balconies, right? We can join them up with these floor boards.' She poked the end of the nearest plank with an iron bar. 'One of you can skate along there instead.'

There was a long pause. Everyone waited to see how everyone else would react.

At last Anthony laughed.

'I ain't getting up there. No one will.'

The others stiffened. Lisa looked pissed off. That summer, Anthony had expanded from reediness into new breadth and height; and it made him cocky. He was bigger than Lisa now. But the others knew she could still do some damage with the bar in her hands. Kim – rash with her earlier success – blurted out,

'I know who'll do it.'

'Who? *You*?' Lisa asked, incredulous.

Kim felt wounded. Her friend's fickleness made her hesitate for a moment. She shook her head, and turned to look over at Eugene, cycling in the playground. His coat was flapping foolishly in the breeze.

'No,' Kim said. 'Him.'

They all considered this possibility.

'He'd do it for a wodge of Caramacs,' Kim said.

'Fourth floor up?' Lisa speculated.

'*Fourth*?'

'Has to be, dope. How would we get into the flats on the first floor?'

'All right… fourth.'

They would need to bridge six balconies across the front of Gooch House. There were twelve planks, each around fifteen foot long.

'We'll nail the ends in,' said Christian. 'Those windows are Kim's... Lisa's... Anthony's... Marcus's... Emma's... mine.'

'Emma's in Weston-Super-Mare,' said Marcus.

'S'all right, her dad left a key with us,' Christian said. 'Me nan's in, by the way.'

This didn't matter. You could tell Christian's nan the planks were for a new conservatory and she'd believe you.

'Someone needs to buy the Caramacs,' Kim reminded them.

'Amanda can get those,' Lisa said. Out came her purse, and Kim thought: *Lisa really wants to do this; she's paying for it.* Yet Amanda – against expectation – rebelled.

'I ain't doing it, Lisa. It's wrong.'

She wasn't putting it on, either; there were real tears in her eyes.

'Don't be such a bleeding wuss,' said Lisa. 'Here's a quid – you better bring me back the change.'

Amanda's fingers closed round the coin but she was properly sobbing and sniffing.

'What's the matter, do you fancy Eugene or something?'

She shook her head violently.

'Get a move on then!'

Amanda shuffled.

'Don't make her,' Marcus said. 'She'll dob us in. Give me the money.'

Lisa prised the pound back from Amanda's fist. Marcus left for the Parade and Amanda was banished to the flat with a slap.

'Little mare,' Lisa said. 'Let's get on with it. Kim, you see if you can get BMX Berkhead over there to agree before Marcus gets back.'

Kim felt almost as reluctant as Amanda. But she remembered Lisa's first expression of approval, and thought about the autumn when they would be back at school. It would be so much easier to have Lisa as a friend. She wavered.

'Can anyone else do it?' A futile question. There wasn't anyone else Eugene would listen to. *No*, he'd say, in that weird flat way he had; just *no*. He wasn't cowed by a slap, like Amanda.

All the same, Lisa wouldn't acknowledge this was the reason. '*You'll* do it,' she said, 'cos I say so.'

Kim assented. She broke away, across the carpark, to the play area. Eugene didn't slacken his speed when she approached.

'I got till dinnertime,' he said.

'I know. We're building a bridge,' she said.

'You what?'

He still didn't slow down.

'From balcony to balcony. Up there. Do you want to ride your bike on it?'

'Dunno.'

'Lisa says she'll buy you some Caramacs. She already sent Marcus to get them.'

'Mom'll buy me lots of Caramacs if I ask.'

And she says Lisa's spoilt, Kim thought.

'A story, then,' she promised. 'I'll tell you a story tonight. You're always saying I won't do that anymore.'

Eugene took so long to reply she thought the conversation might be over.

'OK,' he said finally.

It was midday before all the planks were in place. The boards wouldn't fit in the lift for one thing. Lisa, Kim, Chris and Anthony had to tip-toe on the stairs to avoid detection, which none of them found easy at the best of times. Holding a fifteen-foot plank made silence virtually impossible. Of course they dropped a piece. A crack snaked up the wood grain, but the plank still seemed usable. They put it on the last balcony, between Chris and Emma's. Christian fetched a hammer from his dad's tool kit. Lots of nails were still embedded in the wood. He pummelled them to each balcony ledge.

'That's gonna make a mark,' Anthony told him.

'In for a penny,' Christian said, swinging the hammer with exaggerated force.

Eugene was ready to go by the time they'd finished. Marcus, however, was in trouble; he'd eaten one of the Caramacs on his way back from the shop. Christian twisted his arm round his back so Lisa could root in his pocket for change.

'There's only coppers in here, yer sod,' she said, but she took them anyway. 'I'll keep the chocolate in my bag too.'

'No,' said Eugene. 'Give them to Kim.'

'I ain't got a handbag,' Kim said. 'They'll melt if I hold them in my hand.'

'You have to take them,' Eugene repeated.

'Oh, suit yourself,' said Lisa. 'Come on, the lot of you. We'll get a better view from the car park. Kim, you stop behind and help Berkhead up the plank.'

'Me?' If she stayed alone with Eugene, she suspected she'd stop him. They'd gone too far for that now. 'No. I want a good view, too.'

'Ah, that's snide,' said Anthony, shaking his head. 'Your own brother.'

In this way everyone congregated in the carpark, except for Amanda – who was watching from a bedroom window. Kim could see her peeking over the My Little Ponies on the sill. And, three flats along, there was Eugene.

He looked very small from ground level.

Kim watched her brother walk his bike up the little ramp they had constructed. His audience were half apprehensive, half swaggering that the plan had progressed so far. All the children held their breath as Eugene swung himself on to the saddle. The bike teetered.

'He's gonna fall, he's gonna fall!' Marcus yelped, grabbing Anthony's sleeve and yanking it.

'Shut up,' Lisa said.

The bike straightened. Though the plank was bowing in the middle, Eugene proceeded.

He picked up speed. There was a collective gasp.

'That's amazing,' Anthony whispered.

Eugene was already as far as the second balcony. The sun was at its highest in the sky. Beams flashed on the bike bell. Hour after hour of training on the climbing frame had rewarded him. This platform was wide in comparison. His movement was smooth. Like an alley marble on a polished floor. Eugene didn't look like a boy in a blue anorak. He looked like a god. For a moment, Kim thought – for the first time in a long time – that perhaps the old lie was true: he was Pinket Jack's child.

Kim turned away, nauseated by the sight of Eugene so high. She watched the others instead. They were enchanted. He wasn't a joke anymore. He wasn't BMX Berk. Not now. She supposed she should be pleased. Instead she felt something she couldn't quite name. A sense of being cheated? She had been teased too – because of him, not through any fault of her own – and she wasn't wilful, like him; the others' approval mattered to her. She had colluded to be let in. But she might as well be invisible. Lisa was gawping up at the balconies like everyone else. Eugene would get all the glory. When Kim finally returned her gaze to the sky, her fear and nausea warred with the wish he'd fall off.

Cra-a-ck!

The air snapped as the last plank splintered into a *V.* Eugene's bike veered, flipped vertically — his anorak mushroomed above him — and he let the handles go.

Christian saw his nan loom at the balcony window and he ran from the car park, towards the Parade. Nobody else moved. The smell of urine hit their nostrils; Marcus had wet himself. Only Kim made a sound — a low whine that came from her base of her lungs and ascended into a full scream. She watched Eugene fall. All arms and legs. Like the dolls they dropped from the fourth floor with faded, failing hankies for parachutes. Like a puppet with the strings cut. He struck the awning over the bike shed. Bounced once. Hit the gravel. Kim thought: *His face will be scragged.* And then: *Don't be stupid. He's all twisted in the wrong shape.*

He's dead.

Two, three, four neighbours from the lower floors were looking through their windows now, drawn by Kim's cry. Amanda was first out the door, clutching one of her ponies. Fitzpatrick followed. He shielded his eyes from the sunlight and almost lost his footing in the haste to reach the boy on the ground.

Kim ran towards her brother. The others did not follow her. Fitzpatrick's hands were shaking as he searched for Eugene's pulse. The boy wasn't a god, or the son of one.

'You need to telephone for an ambulance,' he said to Kim. His voice was shaking too.

'I called 999,' Amanda said. She squeezed the lilac plastic in her grip. 'I saw him fall from the window. I called the ambulance. Can I have some chocolate?'

Kim had forgotten she was still holding the Caramacs. They had softened in the heat, but Eugene wouldn't care.

His eyelids were fluttering. Kneeling at his side she felt for the pocket in his anorak.

'Here.' She slipped the bars in his pocket. 'You can have all the chocolate you want,' she said.

He was whispering something. It sounded like the word *flying*.

'He's out of it. What possessed you lot?' Fitzpatrick said. He sounded furious, but his eyes were glassy. 'Why didn't you stop him?'

Kim was still only thirteen and she was not used to seeing men as old and gruff as Fitzpatrick crying. Perhaps it was his tears, rather than his anger, that prompted her into a last-ditch attempt to save herself.

'I did try to stop him.' Her own cheeks were wet now. 'He's… wilful. Just ask my mom.'

Eugene was still saying something. Fitzpatrick leant closer to hear.

'He says…'

Kim waited to be denounced.

'He's sorry. He says… he should have listened.'

Kim feels guilty about a lot of things she did in her teens.

But this, most of all.

Tales From the Bus

JAMILA BARRY

On the 50 driving through Digbeth on a winter afternoon:

A young tracksuited white youth SHOUTING into his phone from the minute we board: SHANNON! WHAT'S GOING ON SHANNON! I NEED THIS MONEY! EVEN DAD WON'T HELP! I'M GONNA GET MY HEAD KICKED IN! SHANNON! WHAT ARE YOU DOING? ARE YOU ON THE STAIRS NOW?

Across the whole front row (I am sitting upstairs like a G, but not at the back, ever, because I'm not really a G and who wants close human contact?) are a group of Asian college girls, in black with huge dark brows and severe dark red lips. They are sharing a single bubble tea and passing around a chic square bottle of NARS foundation one of them has just bought (34.99, not bad! said their Somali friend who joined them for selfies, but she screwed her face up like she would never pay so much). If you are going to travel the Joseph Chamberlain route, get used to these kids. Be patient.

Behind me sit two men, an African guy and an older white guy who is some kind of foreman or manager, and he is complaining in a very tired way about the young men (trainees? volunteers? community service kids?) that he has been trying to work with.

'So he came in this morning and he clearly hadn't had his usual quantity of hash…then he fucked off and came back with a smile, so he went for his FIX…and then he was crumpling paper and wasting supplies…you know that white boy with the cap and the stupid face? Yeah, stupid face, well he was on his phone all the time and I just can't be bothered with them any more…'

Across is a young Arab girl with light green eyes and thick glasses, wearing an Andalus Archery hoodie and a headscarf. I feel like chatting with her but she has headphones on, and really I need to stop talking to strangers. Next to the archer is a Polish girl, with headphones, the volume so high you can hear every word of a Swedish House Mafia track.

Up at the front is a chatty guy, giving Watchtower tracts to some old ladies getting on with their market trolleys, wearing their careful hats and headscarves. '*We publish in 600 languages you know!*'

I want to talk to the old ladies too, I have pent-up granddaughter energy inside me with nowhere to go. I want to hold their hands and carry their bags of mangos and plantain for them. I worry about them being lonely, but I bite back conversation and make notes as we wind our way through the abandoned factories.

A man like a better looking and massiver version of Gru from *Despicable Me*: paisley silk scarf, huge well cut wool overcoat, out of place and taking up space

A chunky Asian emo boy with a green fringe

A woman with a short choppy wig and fur coat, who whisper-sings '*Good afternoon*' before sitting down, and '*Thank you Jesus*' once seated

A man who looks Afghan in a grubby parka, scarf wound round his woolly hat and an ornate silver ring, set with a topaz. He's just missing a glass of tea and a dish of Hunza apricots

An old black lady who just got on with her friend and refused to sit in the empty seat near her, because the seat is warm, 'Make it cool first! Make it cool! Don't want to sit on someone's backside...'

A sleek Chinese girl with a sleek black fold up bike who is dressed entirely in shades of grey and black (my favourite colour palette!). Boyish haircut, black framed glasses, grey and black Nikes. I watch and covet as she opens her grey MK bag with silver studs and pulls out grey fingerless gloves. Black nail varnish, white earphones. Now I feel intrusive, and stop making notes.

Two uni girls in caramel camel coats are talking about their breakfasts. The hijabi girl says she was late up, but her mom made her toast and omelette – her mom can make it so fast! The girl with glasses says how nice her friend's mom is and that she only had 'standard boring jam' on toast. Hijabi says she puts jam on both sides but it makes it hard to hold... Glasses says she puts it on one side and then holds it upside down to eat.

They discuss jam on toast for a long time, before moving on to milk vs soya milk and their student loans.

I could stop listening, but then I'd have to think.

Leaving early for work, my house pulsates with energy behind me, stuffed with responsibilities. In the evening, my children and their cousins are draped around the living room, laughing, arguing, lifting weights, unpicking their braids and playing FIFA and telling me they love me. It's warm and noisy and all the lights are on. I have to pick my way through their detritus to get to the kitchen.

Upstairs there's a broken drawer laid out for my attention. I will be the one searching for plastic widgets in the half dark, moving slowly, still surprised that I'm in charge.

Back in the bus, there's a glimpse of a secret walled garden through an archway. We pass old factories, some just red brick shells. Plants grow out of stone, windows covered with gold and silver foil. We drive past the park with its crowd of tiny red-shorted footballers, spattered with mud. Past the flats where my friend's ex lives with his new family: two adorable round-headed boys in place of his teenagers across town.

Brighton Road, Runcorn, Ombersley, streets we once lived on. This was my home, this was not my home. We pass the school my brothers and I washed up at when we moved from Ireland, fresh from our homeschool collective. I carried a leather satchel and tried to befriend classmates by quoting Groucho Marx.

Coming up to the coach station, there's wasteland by the canal all fenced in with graffitied boards. The spraypainted faces as familiar as family. In summer it's full of buddleias, can you imagine that? Mountains of red brick, covered in purple flowers. If you are waiting at the bus stop on Rea Street on a hot day, you can peer in through the cracks and smell the scent, hear the bees.

With a Wink from an Angel

STEPHEN GOODYEAR

(1937–2021)

Lots of families lived in terraced, backstreet slums around the inner suburbs of Birmingham before the war. Some – like my mother – in the worst of rented hovels, within earshot of factories soon to be working day and night.

The city was the heartland of a smog-blighted industrial Midlands, its diverse industries vital to our nation's well-being. A fact fully appreciated by the Luftwaffe, come the start of hostilities.

Over the lifetime of her marriage, dire straits were nothing new to my mother and moving constantly had been a regular thing, until the war came. When *he* went into the army, for the first time in her married life, she could pay her way.

'Before then I could never get straight,' she'd say, 'paying the rent regular, the way he was, was just not on.'

The fact that my mother's life changed for the better at the start of World War Two gives some indication of how it was before. Just like the arms dealers of the world, she found she had a vested interest in the war – not only because it gave her tabs on our dad's whereabouts (or so she thought) but because with him in the army, it gave her the first chance in her married life to get a real home together: the rent paid each week and her kids properly provided for, is all she'd ever wanted.

And now she had it because what he earned would come straight home and she wouldn't have to find him in the pub on pay day.

I'm sure he'd have dodged the draft if he could but once Dad's call-up papers arrived he exchanged his builder's trowel for a rifle, his work drills for fatigues. At last, he would have to toe the line and with a bit of luck, Mom's life would change too – starting with getting out of the pit where we lived.

And we did, thanks to Alice Thomas.

A decent woman who, in spite of knowing our family's track record with landlords, put us forward for an empty house at the end of a terrace, which backed onto where she herself lived in Hallam Street. Alice recommended Mom, certain that her situation would improve while *he* was away, serving his country.

Through a low garden gate, a short path ran up to the front door, a bay window on its right. There was no hall, the door opened straight into the front room, behind which was a parlour and a little back kitchen. Upstairs, there were two bedrooms and a small box-room, just big enough for a single bed.

Mom was ecstatic with her little house and for good reason: it had its own outside toilet and small yard.

And now Dad was in the army, Mom knew she could take on this dream of a house and meet the rental, without constant worry. She was probably the only person in the land hoping Hitler didn't surrender too soon and end her dream.

She also had to hope that he didn't drop a bomb on it.

I had stopped in my tracks to watch two powerful beams of light criss-cross the night sky, hoping to see the source of the heavy droning noise that approached overhead. Mom's grip on my wrist tightened. Yanking at me, she snapped: 'Come on, we got to get round to Alice's quick or we're going to cop it.'

The entryway through to Alice's backyard was pitch black, its gate shut. My mother was *heavy*, expecting her next – our Rita

— and carrying blankets under both arms. My hesitation unbalanced her and she came close to falling over me.

'Bloody move,' she shouted, as her thigh helped propel me through the blind-dark.

At the shelter, all I could see was a drop into a black hole. Mom's knee nudged me again. A pair of hands appeared, grabbed me and pulled me into the murk. Inside, I couldn't see a thing except when I turned to look back and saw my mother's silhouette as she shouldered aside the canvas draped across the doorway.

She couldn't see a thing either, asking: 'Are all my lot here, Alice?'

A torch shone on the face of her eldest, my then ten-year-old big sister, Linda, whose arms held me snug on her lap. Another torch shone on my brothers, Leslie and Raymond, who sat alongside us. Our dog, Peggy, sprawled across their laps, was licking my knee.

Alice's two big lads, Jack and Henry, were the ones with the torches. Henry leaned over and gave me his, having first showed me how to make a scary face.

I was only minutes into this little distraction when the first deafening explosion occurred, seemingly, right on top of us.

I remember how it shook the place.

How the flash revealed everyone cowering. It was their faces buried in their hands or seeing them with their eyes screwed up tight that sticks with me.

They appeared to expect far worse than I could imagine — I was seemingly detached and unconcerned.

Perhaps I was too young and too dense.

When I told my mother I could remember this and described how my two brothers had their heads bowed and faces hidden against the dog, how Linda's muffled mumblings were at the back of my neck, my mother couldn't believe it. According to her, that night was "horrific" and the kind of nightmare our minds mercifully erase and forget.

Well, mine didn't and I could have told her that I've known far worse and remember it only too well.

'As God is my judge, Alice, I'm telling you not a word of lie,' Mom said later, 'you'll never ever get me and mine down a bleeding death-trap of a hole like that ever again, never. We might just as well perish at home as under the ground.'

But then Mom could always give a tale more thunder than it ever had, especially if it helped her point.

'There you are, look,' Mom said, with relief, as we edged back and saw our house still standing, without a blemish.

To everyone's amazement not a house in our grove had as much as a broken window. Sadly, it wasn't the case for five houses immediately over Alice's back wall, or rather, where her back wall had been.

We could now see into Jakeman Road from our bedroom, through a gap in the rubble. A bedroom wall rose from the debris, a framed picture hanging, intact and in place.

Another ruin still had its upstairs chimney breast and a wardrobe trapped in a corner alcove, a green floral dress jammed in its doors. Alice said it was where her cousin Ada's daughter's best friend lived. She recognised her mother's dress.

Perverse as it sounds, kids in our war-stricken city found much to interest and excite them. My brothers couldn't wait to get out and inspect how the neighbourhood may have altered after each bombing. They enjoyed racing with me in my kiddie's pushchair to take a look. They didn't push the pushchair as such but took turns scooting it backwards in handle-first fashion. With one foot placed between mine on the footplate, they bent over me, bodily holding the armrests as they boot-scooted – usually at a speed and skill not lacking in thrills for its gleeful passenger.

Occasionally they skidded to a halt and peered up at the sky. One brother would hold and angle my head upwards as the other breathlessly pointed out vapour trails, explaining that the tiny specks of metallic glint up there – which I can't honestly say I ever saw – were men in aeroplanes, trying to shoot each other down. I may not have had the nous to know why and must have assumed it was what men in planes did but I was contagiously enthused, just the same.

One day we were with four or five other lads, all bare-kneed in tatty short trousers and all with similar basin-cropped mops, when one of the group remarked: 'Our mom saw a tram lying flat on its side along Bristol Street this morning.'

'S'it still there?' several voices asked.

'Dunno – let's tek a look'

Like a small posse, we raced off, me propelled at the fore. Each lad insisted on taking a turn to scoot "the kid" and would run with me at speed, leaving me free-wheeling between changeovers.

After one long run and push, I was going at a rapid pace down the steeper stretch of Belgrave Road, too fast for any of them to catch up – I had gained the sort of momentum that you expect just before take-off – and then my little wheels met the tram-lines at the Gooch Street crossing. A sharp turn toppled the carriage, propelling me out head-first, my face impacting with the hard stone kerb.

Some fun.

It gave me my first black eye and a slight change to my features: a gash where my teeth cut through the gum above the left side of my upper lip had a long-lasting effect. Tracing it with my tongue, it felt like a second mouth, yet my brothers said it "weren't nothing."

My mother did not concur.

There's another early memory from this time that I can't forget, as much I've tried.

We saw the dead carcasses of two big carthorses in a bombed railway yard at the coal-wharf along Athol Street, off Moseley Road. One horse had been raised in the blast onto a flat railway wagon. Its hefty head lay peacefully but bloody between its splayed legs, while its back legs hung down the side of the wagon, almost touching the ground.

We watched as four firemen pulled it to earth with a rope.

That pitiful looking horse was whole and rigid, like it might have stood up if you could lift it onto its massive hooves.

The other one I only managed a quick glance at before I had to look away.

'Oooogh, look at its guts,' my brother said.

But for once, I'd seen enough.

Elvira Tolland

LAURENCE INMAN

1968. My golden time. The year…

…I was nineteen. The summer of *Hey Jude,* The Troggs telling me that love is all around and Dionne Warwick asking the way to San Jose. I never got to San Jose, but I did get to Digbeth Coach Station a few times. One time in particular changed my life.

Back then…

…even by the health standards of the day, it was pretty disgusting. It attacked your body in four ways: soot, which settled gently on buildings, giving them all, (and your lungs) a coating of black grease; chemical fumes suspended permanently in the air, stinging your eyes and throat; pigeons, squirting, day and night, their gifts of grey-white shit; and lastly, the food they served in the café. But I was doing a fair job of ruining my body anyway.

How it came about. (Be patient.)

That summer I needed a job, anything, to ease my coming months in Manchester, where I didn't do Philosophy at the university. I didn't do Philosophy for most of the year, then started doing it for a week or two in May and June, just before the exams. The rest of the time I drank beer, told lies to women, told lies to anyone just for the hell of it, wrote drippy poetry, played football, acted in plays, went to Eng Lit lectures without being a registered Eng Lit student, and strode around the rainy soot-black city, in a long coat, with a cigarette hanging from the corner of my mouth, pretending to be Albert Camus. Those were the little things I was busy doing, but the big thing I was busy doing was stealing time from myself, the best time from my one-and-only precious life and crushing it up like a scrap of paper, then tossing it into the bin. But even though I ate rubbish, smoked, drank and filled my head with lies, I had a lot of youth and health left and it seemed a fair deal at the time. After three years I got my degree. I've since calculated that if I'd done twenty-eight minutes less work I would have failed.

I was told...

...that the area around Digbeth was a good place to look for a job. I'd find one in no time. They were always looking for people, in little factories and workshops. I was doubtful. But it was true, and Digbeth, the area, the warrens of streets north and south of the main road, was a surprise, an urban treasure hidden from those on the bus heading down to safety in Moseley and Kings Heath.

It was Monday, June 24th 1968...

... a bright sunny morning, as I began my wanderings, starting near the memorial to the Polish officers murdered at Katyn. There were still terraced dwelling houses in that part, but mostly it was small factories, workshops, some of them found up tiny alleys. There were pubs, corner shops, cafes, places selling only sandwiches and tea. It was the last place I remember seeing one of those old cast-iron street urinals.

It's no good asking me now…

…where it was exactly, the factory. I only know it was on the north side, possibly near Alison Street. There were some of those arches nearby under the railway carrying trains into Moor Street. I passed a notice in a small glass case screwed to a narrow door: Tudge and Sons. Makers of Superior Oil Seals and Gaskets. Vacancy. Apply within.

I knocked and heard a quiet voice say, 'Come in.'

Inside was an old man in overalls sitting at a table, sipping tea from a cup and saucer.

'Is this Tudge and Sons? It says outside there's job going.'

'Are you sure you want one?'

'Eh?'

'I always ask that first. The jobs here are very repetitive. You'll get very bored.'

'The money helps though. I should think.'

'Oh, we pay you.' He said this as though there might have been some doubt. 'Are you a student?'

'Yes.'

'What are you studying?'

'Philosophy.'

'That should help.'

We stared at each other for a while.

'Right,' he said, 'we make a range of products here, but you'll be on gaskets. A gasket is a fibre ring, essential to the working of internal combustion engines. They will come down a conveyor belt towards you, all higgledy-piggledy. But they must leave you neither higgledy nor piggledy. They must be arranged so as to make their picking up easier for the two blokes at the end of the belt, whose job is to pack them in boxes.'

'Sounds fairly straightforward.'

'I suppose you'll soon be going back to university.'

'End of September.'

'Three months. That's longer than most people can stand.'

'That bad eh?''

'Young Mr Tudge wanted to modernise things, but he was blown up.'

'What? Here?'

'Oh no. Normandy. On D-Day.'

I was led to a room...

...where, at one end, a conveyor belt emerged through a thick plastic flap covering a hole in the wall, beyond which I could hear a clanking and crashing from machinery, a high whining noise and men shouting things to each other, sometimes quite urgently. There was dust, grease, the smell of oil, cigarettes and sweat.

At the other end of the belt were two young men furiously trying to pack what was on the belt: chaotic piles of gaskets, many of them sliding and spilling to the floor.

'Thank fucking G and J you're here!' they both shouted, almost together.

So, the three of us....

...Me, Col and Den...

...attacked and wrestled and struggled to subdue the never-ending, never-resting ceaselessly-flowing snake-bastard that was Tudge and Son's production of gaskets. After an hour or so we managed to tame it, and even started dealing with the pile on the floor. And then, during our first break, I got to know a bit about my fellow sufferers.

Col was the same age as me. He'd left school at fifteen and been at Tudge's ever since. He was small and stringy with knotty hands and a huge floppy mouth. Den was about four years older, solid and stocky, with a meaty blank face and searching eyes. He'd spent some time in prison. When I asked him what for he said, 'Touching the dog's arse.'

I said, 'Bit harsh.'

But Col explained. 'TDA. Taking and Driving Away. He did it a lot at one time.'

'Yeah,' said Den.

We worked like crazy terriers…

… and in our breaks we slurped mugs of tea and for lunch we ate egg and bacon sandwiches drenched with brown sauce, bought from a café down the street, run by two women in their sixties called Winnie and Mollie. I found out why we had to work so hard.

'It's a six-man job really,' said Den.

'But they put three of us on it,' said Col, 'and pay four and a half men's wages. Normal for round here.'

'I see. So we all win.'

And the wages were very good. Again, it seemed a fair deal at the time. But it took its toll. Col and Den liked a drink. Oh yes.

Every Friday night…

… after being paid we ran off to one of the two dozen or more pubs within half a mile of the factory. They were lovely places: warm cosy little cubby-holes run by men called Wilf or Stan. Men you'd be happy to call your uncle. Or even your dad.

And Wilf or Stan (or Joe, or Bill, or Norm) established a holy, autumnal serenity, a sagacious calm, which settled in every room of their pubs, somehow making it impossible for trouble to develop. We tried a few pubs before settling on The

Lamplighter's Arms, along Floodgate Street. It's called something else now. The Dancing Parrot, I think. And so, for those three months, we fought with the gaskets, we quaffed sweet tea, we stuffed industrial quantities of sausage, bread and brown sauce down our necks, we told lurid stories of the sweaty nights of sex we never had, each of us knowing the others were lying. I loved that summer. I knew I'd always remember it. And all I really had to do to live it fully was be born in 1949. That's got a downside. I'm seventy-four. So far.

The road to the Coach Station. (Nearly there.)

Friday the 27th of September 1968 was my final shift and my final drink with Col and Den. They knew I was off back to Manchester, by coach, the following day.

'What time's your bus?' said Col.

'Two o'clock.'

'Meet us at the Lamplighter's. We'll have a few pints then see you off,' said Den.

On my way to Digbeth that day…

…I made a detour and called at the tobacconist at the corner of New Street and Corporation Street, where, for no other reason than that I loved the blue, smoky, wafty design on the packet, I bought twenty Gitanes.

The three of us had a few quiet pints, a few louder ones, and a few whiskeys in between, and the time just evaporated, and as we stumbled over Digbeth we saw my bus swinging out and off to Manchester without me. So we trudged off back to the pub. Anyone who's ever been nineteen and drunk too much at lunchtime will be able to write the next bit. First, we became noticeable. Then, a little bit annoying. The final phase, as everyone knows, is when you think about setting fire to the curtains, but we managed to stop at The Mad Phrase Stage. This is when a set of words, usually meaningless and inappropriate, floats, separately and independently, into the heads of everyone present, and they feel they have to repeat it, very loudly, over and over and over again. That day ours was GET OUTTA HERE! It came out of our mouths in capitals much bigger than that. We yelled it as we wandered in front of the traffic, screamed it at passers-by, bellowed and echoed it in the grimy shed of the Coach Station. My bus! GET OUTTA HERE! All the window seats were taken. I sat in the nearest available place and glanced at the person who would be sharing my journey.

Oh, she was…

…my age, maybe a year older. Slim. Her face was angular and at the same time smooth. She wore enormous glasses. Black wavy hair tumbled down her back and she was reading. She didn't look up from her book, didn't give me a glance. I sat down and the coach engine chugged alive and I looked across her to what was happening out of the window and of course it was Den and Col acting like complete twats. First they waved their fists and shrieked GET OUTTA HERE! Very loudly, because they thought I wouldn't hear through the window. Then they hooted it like chimps, jabbing their hands under their armpits. Then, because the window was quite high, Col climbed onto Den's shoulders and pretended that he was trapped and drowning in a water tank, smearing his wobbly mouth against the glass, leaving a trail of spit and bubbles.

She looked up from her book, and…

…turned and regarded them, then turned to me and said, 'Would you ask your friends to stop doing that.' It was a stated command disguised as a request, in a voice like her face, soft but edged. I made a what-can-I-do face and smiled weakly at the pair of them, still staggering around, Col still on Den's shoulders. It seemed to go on and on and on, me making faces to them, my life-long mates, clowning and shouting, till the coach edged away into the traffic and that was the last I ever saw of them. Their final words were a faint, echoing GET OUTTA HERE!

In those days you could…

…drink all lunchtime, get on a coach (with no toilet) for a three-hour journey and not want a slash. You could smoke wherever you liked, in other people's houses without asking, or next to complete strangers sitting on a coach and wreath them in foul, reeking fumes from French cigarettes. And I did. Somewhere up the M6 I noticed that the book she was reading was *The Secret Agent* by Joseph Conrad. I looked across and said, 'Great, isn't it?' There was no reaction. I wondered afterwards what she thought I meant. 'Great, isn't it, having to sit next to a sweaty youth smelling of beer and Gitanes?' Later still she turned to the fly-leaf and wrote something. And then I noticed a name written there, in bold, large, forward-sloping handwriting. Elvira Tolland.

Elvira Tolland!

Someone with that name, surely they lived in a vast house in the Irish countryside, where W. B. Yeats visited and fell in love. Surely.

In those days you could not….

…make simple logical links, such as that someone boarding a coach from Birmingham might also be from Birmingham, or that a person going to Manchester and reading a Conrad novel might also be a student at the university. This must be why, when I found myself, six months later, attending a lecture given on *Women in Love* I was astounded to see her again. I followed her to the bar in the basement of the students' union. She was with a group of others from the lecture. I said, 'Hello, Elvira.'

And her face…

… turned and stared back at me and I watched as it slowly filled with the memory of that afternoon. She smiled. She said, 'My name's not Elvira. That must have been the name of the previous owner. I picked it up in a second-hand bookshop.'

I said, 'What a memory.'

'All I did was remember that my name's not Elvira.'

'So what is it?'

'Helen.'

'Close.'

'No, it really is Helen.'

I laughed. She looked at me, remembering one final thing. 'Do you still smoke those disgusting French cigarettes?'

Reader, I did not marry her.

Instead I married her best friend, who was standing nearby. No one knows why, especially not me. It seemed to go with the way my life was. Emphatic beginnings, then a trailing off. Incompleteness. A bit like starting a university course you know nothing about. It was the same for her. It's a very common story. And a very short one.

A dozen or so years went by....

....in which I tried to find a place where I could become the person I had once been, and abandoned somewhere. The threads of chance and circumstance took me to various other cities, here and abroad. And I filled that time, teaching sometimes, trying to be an actor, making and losing money, trying to find the tiny seed of good I could plant in the world. Those threads, seeds, moments, are so fragile. The smallest pressure breaks them. A few seconds here and there, a stroke of a pen, a seat left vacant. We receive a vital message and hardly give it a glance, then just throw it in the bin. And all the time something, someone, is moving, street corner by street corner, pavement by pavement, to join us and keep an appointment which, for all we know, might have been arranged years before.

So, one hot morning in August...

... some decades ago, I was in London, making my way to Birmingham to sort out the sale of my parents' house. They had both died within a year of each other. I could have got a cab to Euston, but I happened to be in Pimlico, it was a nice morning, so I strolled up to Victoria and joined a queue at the Coach Station. And there, two people ahead of me, I saw a familiar tumble of black hair.

'Hello Helen. Going somewhere nice?'

The look on her face as she turned hadn't changed.

'Yes,' she said. 'Home.'

'So am I.'

And we've been here ever since.

Behind Closed Doors

MEAVE HAUGHEY

It was out of the ordinary to measure someone for a mourning suit at their place of work, but it hadn't been convenient to attend the librarian at his home. The reason for this was unclear to Bridget, but it wasn't her place to ask. By the time she and Mr Barker arrived, it had grown late; the arched doors of the library had been pulled shut, and the lending desk and reading room were silent. For a young woman to measure a man was unusual, and these were unusual circumstances, but discretion, Mr Barker explained, was a matter which was sometimes more malleable than it would seem.

It was seamstresses the firm had wanted. The 'Situations Vacant' in the *Mail* Bridget's brother read aloud to her had asked for 'skilled bodice hands'. Bridget had done piecework in front of the cast iron fire with her mam since long before they'd arrived from Ireland and her fingers ached at the thought of it. Even as a child she'd helped her granny; Bridget's tiny hands pricked by the hooked scales of the fuller's teasel as she dragged it across the cloth to raise the nap. She had never been content with that life. Instead, she longed to be one of the presentable young women at Bach and Barkers ready to be sent directly to the homes of the bereaved to measure them for mourning clothes. She knew it might be difficult, but she hated the thought of years spent working long hours by candlelight for meagre wages or in the dirty factories like most of the other Irish girls. Bridget liked the idea of being among the finer things, even if it was at a funeral draper.

It was known that Bach and Barker were the best of the mourning warehouses. They catered for every aspect of bereavement with drapers, milliners, and seamstresses at the ready - even coffins with fashionable ready-made shrouds; in fact, a whole funeral procession. Bridget had seen the handsome feather men with their ostrich plumes, the sombre mutes who walked in front of the horses or stood outside houses paying respects, the midnight black hearse. By a week and a day after a loved one departed, any respectable lady or gentleman would need to enter full mourning, so there was little time to lose - and Bach and Barker were there to assist.

On her first day, Bridget and the other applicants had been met by an elegant saleswoman in floor-length silks who prepared the new girls on the way. The seamstresses were to speak as little as possible, and then to do so only in lowered voices. Bridget's stitching sampler, which she carefully placed next to the others on the leather top of Mr Barker's desk, was accomplished, but he wanted perfection.

'Everything,' he said catching Bridget's eye, 'must be the very best.' As he continued, she studied the imposing figure in his frock coat and cravat, a silk band encircling his tall hat, as he made it understood with flamboyant passion that jet beads were to be fastened to shawls by neat stitches as though the beads themselves were tiny drops of grief. Normally, the other girls said, Mr Barker dismissed unsuccessful seamstresses, sending them back to a life of factory or piecework so it seemed unusual for her to have been chosen. What was it about her character,

Bridget wondered, which suggested to him that she might have a place in the showroom? Strangers had always confided in her, so perhaps she had a trustworthy face, though she wasn't sure if the other girls thought so. They weren't cruel exactly, but they kept their distance.

Her first week in the showroom, she heard Rena and Birdie whispering that she was a pet of his, and it was true. Mr Barker had his best seamstress measure Bridget in black silk and crape and then he himself instructed her the correct way to stand next to the quivering ferns, her face still, and mournful. As the months passed, he attired her in a variety of mantles, lace or kid gloves; sometimes she held a parasol. She was pleased that despite the whispering of the other girls, Mr Barker believed she put the lady customers at ease, and if it was a gentleman on his own, Mr Barker said, he softened somehow with Bridget being there.

Under his guidance she learned to listen to the bereaved with patience, to appear sympathetic, and yet to place in their mind the desire for things which they hadn't before considered necessary: vulcanite chains, bog oak bracelets, brooches, bonnets, crape and muslin collars, pelerines.

When she had perfected that skill, she began to accompany him on visits to the homes of the bereaved. It was good, he said, to have a woman there with the lady fitter so as to put the family at ease. Bridget listened as though moved and encouraged people to be comforted by some of the more frivolous items from the catalogue she always carried on her lap in the carriage.

Bridget was glad to be called away with Mr Barker that afternoon. Much of the morning had been spent attending a woman whose husband had died inconveniently young. The poor young woman was still in the first flushes of love, and so it had been easy to suggest the newest and most fashionable ways to pay tribute to her grief. Bridget suggested item after item, each one so readily accepted by the young widow that guilt began to embroider itself along the edges of Bridget's conscience even before Rena and Birdie hissed that it was wrong to take quite so much advantage, given the tragic circumstances. Bridget was aware of wanting to please Mr Barker, who had bristled with pride from across the showroom, watching her with predatory focus. It was like a game between them, and as she talked the young widow into more and more, she found herself drawing a strange pleasure from the audience.

When it was all over, however, Bridget found the experience had quite unnerved her. She stepped outside hoping to clear her head and encountered not only the acrid smells of autumn, but a dark-eyed man standing alone in front of the shop. His scholarly woollen suit and waistcoat appeared far too warm for the weather as though he had just arrived from some frigid corner of the earth and yet his skin was pale. He stared at Bridget through cracked spectacles, his uncanny demeanour rooting her to the spot. Then he opened his mouth as if to speak but no sound issued, for at that very moment, Mr Barker appeared, and met the man's gaze with ill-concealed horror before he hurriedly ushered Bridget inside. There was no time for him to explain, as she was urgently required to attend to the next customer.

It wasn't far from the mourning warehouse on New Street to the double-gabled gothic frontage of the Free Library at Deritend. The gleaming horse with its ostentatious black feather plume was fit and swift and the gig was comfortable, steered by the coachman who brandished a black crape bow on the end of his whip. Bridget sat across from Mr Barker, catching his eye from time to time but saying nothing. Away from the customers, she had learned, he was a man with whom you could sit a long while before he spoke, but Bridget didn't mind. Although there were things she wanted to ask him, she told herself there was a kind of intimacy in that unspeaking.

As they passed down Digbeth High Street toward Heath Mill Lane, the hoots of the factory bells screamed time to finish. Outside the carriage, the late November afternoon was filled with colliding sounds of hammers, guns, metal presses, and the stench of tanning and offal, the reek of lacquer from the Japanning works. Workers poured from the factories into the ale houses or disappeared down the narrow streets which crisscrossed the district to form its labyrinth of factories, workshops, and courts. Every side street, packed with the tiny shops of smiths and knifemakers, rang with the accompanying screech and heat of metal being worked. Even from inside the gig, Bridget could feel grit entering her throat and nose with every breath she took. She thought of her father, coming back from the laquerworks, coughing powdered glass into his handkerchief, his pale blue eyes lined with pigment that settled into his wrinkles, mapping them like tiny rivers traced in ink.

Bridget knew he was frightened for her mam: she was too. The visitors came more often now. Da said they were ghosts, who surely foretold death, or danger. But it was only failing vision playing tricks on the mind, the oculist explained, holding a candle up to mam's milky eyes, and no amount of the physician's leeches or the apothecary's tinctures, tonics, or general cure-alls would change things. Mam stopped being able to stitch, to do the close, detailed work she had always done. What good, she said desperately, was a woman who couldn't work or keep house? Bridget had had to find better work and though she could hardly admit it, she dreaded coming home to where Mam reached helplessly for things, trying to read whether they were real, or only shadows.

The gig slowed as they neared their destination. As Bridget watched, Mr Barker's face changed, his expression ready to greet people with his theatrical charm. He hadn't spoken during the journey, his face inscrutable as ever, but his fingers worried the edge of his coat as though he were unusually troubled, and Bridget felt sure he was still thinking about that morning and the man outside the shop.

Mr Barker knocked, and there was a long pause where they stood still and silent as though time had stopped for them alone. Bridget felt night wrap round her, as it filled with the smudge of coal fires from The Crown, the damp of the Rea, the sweet warm smell of the coachman's horse. The edge of the sky lost distinction against the blue brick railway viaduct which loomed high across Heath Mill Lane. She remembered the sky over the homeplace in Ireland, one night coming down the lane in her father's arms through fields of tiny white flowers, the stars at once overhead and underfoot, the Milky Way like skeins of wool – and she tried to recall the song her granny used to sing to her when the world was wild and green.

But then at last the sound of locks turning, the great creak of the doors and there, his dark eyes fixed on them, was the man from outside the shop that afternoon. This time it was he, the librarian, who urged Bridget and Mr Barker inside, Bridget's mind suddenly wondering whether she had misunderstood. She wanted to ask Mr Barker, to know why he caught her eye with a look she couldn't fathom, but almost at once the gentlemen moved out of earshot and Bridget was left to wait.

Bridget had often imagined herself in the churchlike silence of the Reading Room. She'd mithered her brother, a clerk at a nearby works, until he had described it to her. She envied Brendan sitting reading the papers with the other men. It seemed, to Bridget, that news of the outside world only came to women through men. Barred from the Reading Room, she would instead queue to look through the thick catalogue on the lending desk or pretend to fill in a card requesting this or that. Often, she dawdled intentionally so that when the door swung open she caught a glimpse of men lent over McCullough's *Dictionary of Commerce* or Taswell-Langmead's *English Constitutional History*, or leafing through the pages of Seeley & Etheridges *Textbook of Geology* at the long leather topped tables, or standing turning the pages of *The Echo, The Times,* or *The Birmingham Journal* under the light from the pair of angled windows in the roof. And although she could sense the annoyance of the moustachioed lending desk assistants with their round glasses and waistcoats, she feigned interest in the catalogue, all the while glancing at the wooden door beyond marked 'Librarian's Room'. She hoped it would one day open to her, revealing a desk covered in important papers, a cup of tea nestled among them, the stacks beyond.

The light from the long lantern window in the open-timbered roof dimmed as late afternoon disappeared into early evening. As they moved further into the room, Mr Barker and the librarian became indistinct from the shadows. It was unlike Mr Barker to leave her for so long and so alone. Still Bridget waited, submerged in the narrow patch of light which reached through the small window in the gable end.

With the librarian and Mr Barker rapt in muffled conversation, Bridget carefully stepped sideways into the reading room and stretched her hands to touch the wall, running her gloved fingertips across the ridge and furrow of the wooden roller shutters which had been pulled down over the shelves and locked. She was fascinated by the keyholes which looked back at her, their decorative eyes silvered and floral, blinking back the secrets of the volumes beyond. From where she stood, the door to the Librarian's Room was tantalisingly close. It rested slightly ajar, revealing a row of keys on hooks. There must be one, the curved bow of its handle decorated with wreaths of tiny flowers, that fit into the sliver of lock. It would only take another few steps, she thought, and the key would be pressed into the palm of her gloved hand. She could almost feel the pressure of the key in the barrel as it urged the mechanism open, then hear the click, and the rumble of raising shutters.

Mr Barker and the librarian were out of sight, their distant voices lowered in a way which suggested they still had much to discuss. Bridget saw her chance. She crossed the entrance hall and ducked through the door into the Librarian's Room. Within moments the key was in her pocket. She wrapped her fingers round it as though, if by clasped tightly enough, it would tell her what to do next. She stood for a moment, marvelling at the space – tall bookcases full to the high ceilings, wooden ladders which could be drawn from side to side along a brass railing, large volumes with beautifully embellished covers stacked neatly on the pedestal desk. If only it were that easy, she thought. If only she could draw a chair up to the desk and spend her life learning about all the places and things in her imagination. She thought of her mam, and her granny before her, working themselves into an early grave and wondered what they would make of her, standing amongst the learned smell of leather and paper, a stolen key in her pocket. But even as she stood, the muted colours of the leather spines vanished into the encroaching dark and she heard disagreement, and the sound of footsteps approaching.

But it was not Mr Barker who appeared, rather the dark-eyed librarian on his own. He came close to her then, close enough that she could not avoid the musty smell of his suit as he illuminated a small lamp and insisted that she begin.

Where, Bridget wondered, was Mr Barker?

Taking up her tape, she turned her head to the side, trying, for propriety's sake, to avoid resting it against the librarian's body as she reached with both hands around his waist. He was silent as she drew chalk lines to mark seams down his back, and his arms, trying to steady her hands which shook with fear. Although he made almost no movement, he meant her harm, she was certain of that. His presence was like a weight which pulled Bridget down, drowning her in darkness. Then, he faced her, his rigid figure stretched into shadows which reached up to the ceiling and she felt his eyes surveying her as the thin paper measuring tape encircled his neck, drawing tight to the buttonhole.

'I hope', he said, 'you are not too tired from waiting on my poor wife this very day'.

His mottled hands opened his collar and Bridget saw with horror a line of stitches sewn into his blueish flesh like the train tracks that followed the canals.

White Car

GARRIE FLETCHER

I stepped onto Heath Mill Lane as the car came round the corner. It caught me below the knee, flipped me onto the windscreen and left me on the road as it sped away under the viaduct. The heat of the day radiated out of the tarmac into the night. I lay in the lane, my left cheek flat against asphalt, breathing in rubber and exhaust fumes. Despite blood running into my hair and eyes, I started to laugh – it looked just like her car. Just like the crappy Fiat Punto she bought when she got the job at the Yorkshire Post, that shitty, white, rattling box on wheels. And, whenever I think back to it now, I see her driving through me outside The Old Crown, her black hair piled up on top, eyes sharp, focused, red lips curving up into a bitter smile that says, got you. Got you, you fucker.

I can't one hundred percent say it wasn't her, but it seems unlikely that she'd risk her glittering career in online advertising just to wipe me out.

I've no idea how long I was waiting. It didn't feel that long, but time was elastic and sticky like the blood in my hair. The triage nurse looked tired. Dead tired. I went to put my arm around her, but she batted my hand away with weary expertise. Stitches and rest. Concussion. Definitely concussion. I had to wait until someone was free – it would be a long wait. Up until this point, everything had happened so quickly, even the slow bits. I went back to the waiting area and sat down next to Mum. It seemed natural that she would be there, but I'm sure she wasn't before I went in. The times she wasn't there she was outside smoking. I told her the cigs would kill her and she said she'd live longer than me at this rate. This was the first time I remember looking at her and thinking she was old. She was still a good-looking woman; you could see echoes of the girl she'd been, but they were getting harder to make out hidden by lines and wrinkles. I held her hand for a bit. It didn't seem odd at all.

Me and the lads had been drinking since seven. The Digbeth Loop. Starting at The Anchor then up Bradford Street to The White Swan down Alcester Street to The Spotted Dog across Digbeth High Street to The Old Crown then, traditionally, along to The Big Bulls Head. Jeff had shouted something about being slaves to tradition and insisted that we throw off our chains and go to The Ruin instead.

The Punto moved in slow motion as if its tyres had started to melt into the road. It came around the side of The Old Crown and I watched as an observer, remote, removed, safe. The undeniable power of drink had slowed time itself and made me invulnerable.

Memory is weird. Memory is finickity, unfaithful, unflinching, and easily smudged by alcohol, but either everything decelerated, and I had time to note and reflect upon what happened as it was happening, or my ability to process what happened sped up to the extent that it had the same effect: time crawled. As the car's bumper hit my shin, flipping me head-first towards the windscreen, I noticed a patch on the bonnet where the paint had peeled off and rust had set in. It looked like a bird. A bird,

I thought, and even as I thought that, I could see that my head was about to crack against the glass and there was nothing I could do about it.

I nudged Mum, 'See her?' I nodded towards a slim woman, mid-twenties with a perfect bob, a tight white blouse and a dark skirt that just about stopped her from being arrested. 'God, I could fuck her.'

The slap was swift, precise and painful.

'I think I've definitely got concussion now.'

'You'll have more than concussion if you carry on like that.'

Now, I'm fairly certain Mum hit me round the face because I used the F-word. At the time, with the bruising, inside and out, and the alcohol, I thought it was because the woman's blouse was covered with blood.

'Yeah, you're probably right. She'd need to change her top'

Faces looked down as I lay in the road. I wondered why these people found me so interesting. A strange blue light flicked across the viaduct brickwork and surrounding buildings. Someone ordered everyone back, and a paramedic knelt beside me. In the back of the ambulance, I calmly and confidently told them my address was 64 Loughrigg Street, an address I'd not only not lived at for years, but that was in a completely different city. It was where we'd lived. It was where I'd painted the table with a red gloss and she'd slowly peeled it off.

The Anchor had been busy, but we'd managed to get a table in the main bar. Pool balls clicked and clacked against each other as a group of kids strutted their stuff trying to impress some indifferent girls. Krish was holding court behind the bar, one of his eclectic playlists soundtracking our drinking. Loz brought the beers back and gently insulted us all, calling into question our ability to hold our drink and our sexual orientation – standard conversation openers.

Jeff drifted over to the indifferent girls in full lounge lizard mode and Loz got into an animated discussion with a bus driver about something. This left me at the mercy of Craig. I've known Craig years. He's one of my oldest friends, but, since his dad, he can be hard work. He'll talk to you, and only you, in an intense flurry of words as if he's trying to offload every thought he's ever had before he forgets. There's a rhythm, slow at first, gradually building until it breaks like waves on the shore followed by a lull as the tide sucks out. This lull isn't to allow you to respond. The lull is intended to allow what's been said time to sink in. Conversations with Craig are draining and confusing.

'I'm the wrong side of thirty and nothing to call my own, not even a fuck buddy, an empty bed in a shared house, mince stolen from the fridge and no fucker owning up, a cooker with only one working ring and a gas bill in the form of a ransom note, mice scratching at my thoughts keeping me awake all night, car headlights across the ceiling and the girl downstairs crying.'

'Craig, can we not do this?' The eyes. The long stare. 'Can we just get pissed and talk shite?'

'You miss her, don't you?'

Mum squeezed my hand so tight that when I looked at it the knuckles had all gone white. When I asked her why she'd done it she said, you know. I didn't, but I wasn't going to push it.

She continued, 'I shouldn't be here. You're thirty-two, nearly thirty-three. Why am I sitting with you in A and E on a Saturday night when I should be at home moaning about rubbish on the telly? You can't keep doing this.'

I'd never done this before, but I wasn't that concussed that I thought pointing that out was a good idea.

There was a roar of laughter from the indifferent girls, and Jeff, in as cool a way as his six-foot-plus gangly frame would allow, sauntered back to our table. He shrugged off their laughter as cultural differences. What those differences were, he would not elaborate on. I noticed, over Jeff's shoulder, that his failed wooing had acted as an icebreaker between the indifferent girls and the pool kids – they seemed to be getting on famously now. I tried to point this out to Jeff, but he pretended he couldn't hear.

Craig turned to the others – the bus driver had retreated to one of the other rooms, brow-beaten by Loz's encyclopaedic knowledge of all things pointless, no doubt – and declared that I was still missing the 'Bradford Girl'. She wasn't from Bradford – I'd met her there – but the title had stuck. Jeff leapt on this chance to move on from his failed advances.

'Stu, it's been over three years. Move on.'

I thought I'd grow old with Bradford Girl. That we'd slowly ferment into something stronger, reliable, permanent. I imagined sitting together on a bench in Lister Park feeding the birds, but there was too much imagining and not enough doing. After a while, her hand never felt right in mine.

I have no idea what happened in The Swan or The Spotted Dog which is weird as I couldn't have been that drunk. There's the sound of a slap, almost a crack that I can't shake like the time the landlady at The Dog reprimanded Jeff with a powerful swipe of her open palm. Jeff blamed that on football and the uneven legs of the stool he was perched on. The landlady blamed it on too much IPA and Jeff's unshakable belief in his affinity with women. He wasn't barred so maybe there's something in it?

In The Crown we were kings. Holding court, proclaiming rulings on everything from the latest self-inflicted, inexplicable, hateful bullshit from our zombie government to the state of Shanaz's quiff. Shanaz had been working the bar at The Crown for a few months now, long enough to feel like she'd been there forever. We watched her hair in all its glory, extended out horizontally from her hairline a good five inches or more, dark and lustrous with product, gently bouncing with each nod of her head as she chatted to someone. And then Loz asked why I'd come back to Brum.

'It's ancient history.'

'He had to be back where the action is. Breathe in the Digbeth night. Gaze at the stars through the legs of the Moor Street viaduct.'

'I did and I stayed because there's something about this place. I feel like we all belong here. We could've been anywhere in the world but we're here...'

'Don't rub it in.'

Whatever else was said was lost in the noise of the pub, the swirl of the Guinness and the throb of my head. Was that now or then? Someone said something about Craig's dad - it may have been me — and we were in danger of slipping into the dark sludge of morbidity, so Jeff declared to Hell with tradition and insisted that we all go to The Ruin instead of The Big Bulls Head.

Mum picked some invisible fluff off her jeans and said she was going out for a fag. I watched her walk out of the hospital, still feeling the ghost of her hand clasped tightly around mine.

Craig's dad had lost his face, and swiftly after, his mind when a gun exploded on his workbench. He worked at the Birmingham Proof House tucked away down Banbury Street between the arches of the London line, all security bars and electronic gates. We'd rarely venture as far east as The Woodman pub before this but never again afterwards, as it would mean walking past Banbury Street and crossing the canal where they found Craig's dad face down two months after the accident.

I touched my face, my nose bigger than I remembered.

'In here, Mr Franks.'

She led me to a cubicle. Told me someone would be with me shortly and then left, swishing the curtain behind her. I listened to my breathing for a bit. It took me a while to realise it was mine. A male nurse flapped through the curtain as if he was being hounded by unseen demons and told me to relax. Easier said than done. He set about putting me back together. I felt the stitches pull through my skin like thoughts turning in and over on themselves. Bradford Girl, white car, work, shitty house, work, white car, Bradford Girl. I couldn't feel Mum's hand anymore. I couldn't feel the stitches.

They let me go.

Said to keep an eye on the pain, paracetamol, ibuprofen. If it gets worse come back, yada yada yada. Mum magicked a taxi from somewhere, old-school, no Uber, and we headed east from the Q.E. back to Balsall Heath. It didn't bother me we weren't heading to mine. Shitty house would still be there when I needed it, but for now, I needed home, real home, not some arsehole's pension plan crammed with losers like me. I lay my head back as the cab made its way through the streets, my head gently rocking and swaying, bhangra faintly playing on the radio, and I pictured the rust bird on the white car's bonnet. As I flipped over towards the windscreen, just before my head cracked into the glass, I saw a raven.

'Do you ever hear from her?'

'Who?'

'The girl. The one in Bradford. Had a funny name, crow something.'

'It wasn't crow.'

'Jenny?'

'I thought it was me who was concussed?'

'Nice girl. You should've made a go of that.'

'I tried.'

'Really? You're too much like your dad.'

'That's not fair.'

'Prove me wrong. There's still time.'

'Is that what it's about? Proving you wrong?'

'It's always been a fight with you, Stu. Ever since you were little, your arms and legs rigid with determination as you sat in your high-chair, desperate to feed yourself...'

'Can we stick to examples from this century.'

'Or your sarcastic comments every time me or your dad tried to help you. It can be draining, despite how much I love you.'

We both let that one hang for a bit. The taxi driver coughed into his fist, making it feel like the whole world knew how infrequently the 'L-Word' was used in our house. How a quick ruffle of my hair or an uncomfortable stare from Mum, lips pursed, almost curving into a smile, would be the closest we ever got to signs of affection. Dad struggled with it and shielded himself with alcohol, armwrestling and car maintenance, occasionally administering a slap on the back and an 'I'm proud of you' when it all became too much.

'I'm too old to be still worrying about you, Stu.' The taxi slowed to a stop at the red traffic lights in Moseley Village, the driver's music too quiet to kill the silence. 'You're thirty-two and still getting pissed with your mates. Still getting into fights.'

'It was a car, Mum.'

'It's always a car.'

I wasn't sure if she was talking about me or Dad at this point. I let the swelling in my head and the alcohol work their magic and drifted into a light sleep soundtracked by dancing girls in full Bollywood regalia.

The slam of the taxi door woke me. I eased my way out of the car, thanking the driver, and joined Mum at the front door as she rummaged for the keys in her handbag. She unlocked the door and looked at me. She didn't look tired; she didn't look angry. She smiled, a real smile, not an approximation learnt from watching others, but a warm, genuine smile, and she led me into the lounge, sat me on the couch and said, 'What are we going to do with you?'

I didn't have a clue, and that was fine. Real fine. A white car ploughed through me and left me for dead, but I was still here and that was something.

It was everything.

On Dereliction and Hubris

CHARLIE HILL

I work on a HelpDesk at Birmingham City University, where I am paid to be friendly. The university is next to Millennium Point, the 'largest landmark millennium project in England outside the capital'. Millennium Point 'enables its visitors and clients to explore ideas, science, education, and technology' and is an integral part of the city's Knowledge Quarter. Birmingham City University used to be Birmingham Poly. I have never fully understood the sense of pride people derive from their place of birth; although I am proud of BCU's School of Art, School of Jewellery, School of Acting, School of Architecture and Birmingham Conservatoire, it has recently expanded its operations by opening a campus in the United Arab Emirates.

The other day, I left work and was walking past Millennium Point when I was accosted by three men. They wore torn clothes and their shoes had holes in and they looked as though they had just shuffled through the Californian dustbowl. They stood in front of me and although they seemed shifty, they were too hollowed out to cause me any physical concern.

One of the men muttered something but I'm half-deaf and didn't catch it. 'Say again?' I said and he muttered something else and pointed over my shoulder. 'What was that, mate? Dog kennels? You want a dog kennel?'

He gave me a look that I didn't want to engage with.

'No, not dogs!' he said, 'food bank! Is there a food bank up here?'

The trains that used to go to London from Birmingham left the city over a half a mile of exquisitely engineered Victorian viaduct. You can see the viaduct from BCU, from Millennium Point. Its arches are serene in their permanence, and they seem symbolic somehow, of myths that may only have existed in the past and have long since lost their pull: pride in your work, a sense of community, collegiate and even transnational endeavour. Beneath the arches is Digbeth. Digbeth was once a tightly packed square mile of redbrick factories and the thriving, bustling pubs and cafes and betting shops of working people. There were Screw Works and Pressed Steel Works, a tea factory, a factory making custard powder, a library and schools. By the side of busy canals sat warehouses. Now most these warehouses are empty; the odd metal spinner or galvaniser excepted, the factories are falling down, windowless and graffitied. Now the district's activity centres on craft ale bars, the odd art gallery and studio, studs of Knowledge Quarter/Creative Content Hub/Enterprise Zone/Big City Plan investment in a rubble-strewn wasteland.

Under a viaduct arch, five minutes from BCU and Millennium Point, is a half-roofed two-storey Victorian factory – PREMIER PLATING TIGS "THE FINISH STARTS HERE"; W.R. PAR INNER SHEET METAL WORKER ESTD 1921 – that sleeps a bevy of the homeless. A couple of years ago I went to a discussion about pan-Europeanism in the Walker Building, a repurposed warehouse round the corner. Down the road there is a pub called Nortons which boasts 'Not Another Irish Bar'. This is an absurd thing to have on a sign in Digbeth – in Digbeth! – whether you are being ironic, or playful, or not.

The Birmingham bit of HS2 is being built in front of BCU and Millennium Point, alongside the Victorian arches. The backstreets that are home to the galleries and empty units and derelict buildings of Digbeth are being torn up, wire mesh fencing erected, taken down, erected again. There is lots of signage proclaiming the glory of the development and the benefits it will bring; none that mention it will stop at Crewe. They are also digging up Digbeth High Street, building tramlines. I'm not sure where the trams will go to but although it will be nowhere like Digbeth – because there is nowhere like Digbeth – it will also be somewhere exactly the same.

One day, cycling to work along my ever-changing commute, I came to a fence across the road, a diversion along a very short stretch of pavement and a sign saying 'Cyclists Dismount!' There is never anyone around at that time in the morning so I ignored it, and mounted the pavement for 3 seconds or so. Someone in a hi-vis jacket shouted something at me from behind a fence, but I didn't catch it. The next day, at the same spot, half a dozen hi-vises blocked my path. There was no-one else around and the stretch of pavement was empty. 'Do you see that sign?' said a big fella, in my face, 'I want you to get off your bicycle.'

At work, I printed a sign of my own. It said 'BULLYING JOBSWORTH CUNT!' in big letters, and on my way home I hung it on the section of fencing next to 'Cyclists Dismount!' For the next two months I took a longer route to work, and reflected on what people would think of HS2 and the tramlines in 150 years' time. It seems there is an historical/ahistorical inevitability to the dereliction of all things that Digbeth's performative hubris won't help.

But then maybe that's just me.

Ghost

KIT DE WAAL

Cheap phones break easily. You can be lying in bed reaching for the tissues to blow your nose – sore, dripping, blocked – and knock a glass over, maybe, a full glass. You can saturate a cheap phone, ruin the mechanism. Or you nudge the phone off the bedside table and the screen cracks, my number lost forever.

One day, you can be kissing someone on Digbeth High Street, a sudden curl into a waiting mouth, shaken by the ardour, people staring (we're not young, after all) and the next you can be – he can be – too ill to raise his head. He could press the buttons but he's too weak to wait for an answer. He doesn't realise how quick I would be. Two rings and I'd pick up.

His eyelids are pasted shut with mucus, with drops from the doctor. Home visit. Too contagious for the waiting room. With crusted eyes you can't see the phone at all never mind use it.

They've taken him to hospital – the neighbours – worried about not seeing him for days. In his delirium, he mutters my name but the nurses have bandages to change and monitors to monitor.

Moved to intensive care now. His friends gather, shocked at his weight loss, in and out of sleep, the morse code of my name tapped with anaemic fingers on a white sheet. But they never met me and don't know the rhythm of my name. His cheap phone, in a hospital locker (cracked, remember and wet inside), does not ring so they cannot answer and explain.

'I'll call you later,' he said, after our Digbeth kiss thirteen days ago. But he caught the flu, was run over, broke his arm, gangrene set in, then sepsis on the ward, then inflammation of the eyes that spread to the brain.

My dead boyfriend is buried without me, he won't ring now. He can't.

Earworm

TOM MAGUIRE

There's a song stuck in my head. It's a crooning disco tune filled with soaring strings and horns. It's an R&B track telling me I have to survive. It's some droning drum and bass punctuated with the *thump* and *fwap* of kick and snare. It's all of them at once, crawling through my ears.

Earworms. That's what Howard called them. Little wriggling repetitive things which excrete the same noise over and over. Make you scratch at your head, open your mouth trying to name the song. Because it's so obvious, isn't it? It's just on the tip of your tongue.

Ahead of me, what's left of Howard stumbles through the Curzon Street tunnel. The canal sloshes and dribbles gently to his right, dampening the wet slap of his footsteps. He's wearing our usual uniform: dark overalls, now scuffed with layers of dust from his endless wandering. Beneath the muck, I can still detect the unmistakable gloaming quality of the fabric. How when viewed at a certain tilt it refracts the light *just so*, throwing off sudden bursts of colour. Each shade thrown seems to go deeper than red or brighter than violet, hurting my head if I look too long.

I'd felt silly when I first put on the uniform. Like I wore a costume meant to entertain a child, dressing myself up in a beetle's iridescent shell.

"You have to, Laura," Howard had said in response. "It puts us halfway in their world. Bosses call it *lo-vis*. Makes collecting them easier."

He's no good at collecting anymore – though he has gained other talents. Since he disappeared, I've only ever seen him in the distance and he's always given me the slip. This is the closest I've come to him in weeks.

I have to catch him tonight. Knock some sense into him. Bring him back to who he was. I don't care how difficult or impossible it seems. I won't give up.

I follow, pausing occasionally to gather the worms that cling to the walls. They are plump, stocky and quivering. Fattened from the clamour of the day's construction, the endless cleaving of the earth to make way for the new train line. I grab them by the fistful. Their dark, ringed bodies turn in my hand. Above, hundreds more of the things hang from the top of the tunnel, suckling still on the ambient noise of traffic. My bag's already filling up.

The tunnel's dark mouth yawns around us. Howard's overalls bristle with movement, apparent even from a distance. The rustle and flex of tiny, strong things straining against their cage. I no longer understand what he is.

He crouches and fiddles with something I can't see. A glut of worms disgorges to the floor, sleek with mucus.

'Oi!' I shout in the most authoritative voice I can muster. He does not turn. 'Howard!'

Still nothing. I start after him and his shuffling gait becomes disjointed with uncanny speed.

My foot catches on something and I tumble forward, scraping my knees and hands on the ground. The worms on the nearby wall undulate, excited by the echoing sound. Behind is the thing that tripped me: a homeless man buried into his sleeping bag.

His feet dangle over the walkway's lip, grazing the water.

'Watch it,' I say. I kick the sleeping bag. 'You can't stay here, you know. Someone could get hurt.'

The bag unzips, revealing a swatch of eye, a lock of sandy hair. 'And where is it I should move to?'

'Not my problem. Shift it.'

The homeless man unfolds from his cocoon and begins collecting his stuff together. I know I should feel a little bad, but I don't. They're always taking the piss. Getting in the way. I'm sick of it.

When I look up, Howard has disappeared around a bend. I sprint through the tunnel mouth, framing the noise of Digbeth at dusk, but he's already gone. My bag clatters with the sound of a thousand jackhammers and my head fills with song-snippets. I wonder what's going on between my ears. Whether I've become a breeding ground for the slithering bastards.

It took me a while to get the hang of the job. It wasn't what I expected when the recruitment agency offered me a role in public sanitation. I'd assumed I'd be litter-picking, changing the bins, riding around in those little street-sweepers which rattle and drone over the city's skin every dusk and dawn.

It was nothing like that. No interview aside from an online questionnaire. A week later, the company mailed me my *lo-vis* overalls along with a reinforced duffel bag and a set of earplugs. They came with a letter telling me to wait at the top of Bradford Street that Friday for my first shift.

That was how I met Howard. He was soft faced with kind eyes. Recently divorced, about ten years my senior. Ours was a *special job,* he said. Hush-hush. Off the books. I think he was trying to make it exciting. He could probably see my disappointment; I didn't really hide it well. I wanted somebody my own age who

I could chat and natter with – not that I had much to chat about. No boyfriend, no hobbies. Don't get on with family. Granted, there were a few friends but I saw them rarely. Most were married off, cloistered away in the suburbs.

I think, in retrospect, that was why we began to bond. It was our shared lack, the void at the centre of our personal lives. Like we were empty jars waiting to be filled.

There wasn't much time for talk at first. He focused on showing me how to see the worms. The way they collected in crevices, hung off ceilings and walls. He taught me how to focus my eyes *just so* until our world upended into theirs. My perception adjusted in increments and their fat, peristaltic bodies rose up like flowers in a foggy field.

I suddenly understood why there were certain patches of pavement where nobody stepped. Certain corners of clubs that would remain empty no matter how packed it got. Most simply edited the worms from their minds, letting them fester in speakers and cluster at the edges of thumping floors without notice or remark. Not me. Not anymore. They were burned into my perception like blemishes on an overexposed photograph.

They tended to disperse during the day. To burrow around in construction sites or hunker down near roads. We gathered them at night as they coalesced around clubs, bars, restaurants. By dawn, we'd typically fill two bulging duffel-bags with the things and it still wouldn't be enough to make a dent.

The first few shifts seemed an unreal dream. But it soon became as everyday as washing the pots or brushing my teeth before bed. Habit will do that, I suppose.

He warmed to me once it was clear I wasn't going to quit as so many others had. He opened to me, unfurling slowly, his voice always a low rustle. Told me about his messy separation from his wife. Asked me about my life, which I found refreshing. A low bar, I know, but not many people have been bothered to clamber over it. We'd complain equally like we'd been assigned some kind of quota. I'd whine my pay was shit and there was nothing good to watch on telly and I couldn't find any new music that I liked. He'd go on about nobody respecting him. How our bosses refused to meet him, only ever messaged to deny his requests for better equipment or higher wages.

We first slept together out of boredom, I think. I'm unsure if either of us enjoyed it, particularly, but it wasn't bad. It at least gave our night-time forays a certain pleasant tension. Shared looks and grazed hands and cheeky smiles as we worked in silence, plastic foam plugging up our ears, muffling the world.

I questioned the purpose of our work only once. I was tangled in his musty bedsheets, my head resting on his tattooed arm. Not ideal as pillow talk, but it had been bothering me. I could tell our job was a kind of sterilisation. We swept up the worms as surely as the police swept up the drunks and the homeless, keeping the city as clean as we could. But I still couldn't fathom what our end goal was. Why it was so important that we collect up those strange, wriggling creatures.

'I struggle to see what harm they're doing,' I said. 'Nobody even notices them.'

'Nobody notices carbon monoxide until it's too late,' was his response.

It was about then that the songs started cropping up. I would hum the same chorus incessantly while I showered. Single sung words ran rampage through my mind while I tried to concentrate on the telly. Errant basslines wobbled out of the aether, came marching straight from Suki10c or The Mill to rest in the folds of my ears.

I wore earplugs religiously, whether working or not. Began scratching at the sides of my head. Blinking harder. Filling my inner world with thoughts, sentences, anything that didn't have a tune or rhythm. None of it worked.

'You see?' Howard said, after the first month. We were sat in his car, the windows fogged. Tendrils of steaming tea danced from my thermos. His belt hung slack on his legs, unbuckled. 'This is their danger. They're parasites. They sit, gobbling up whole songs and sounds, and they shit out the bits and bobs they can't digest. Pump it through the air all around us. Stinking fragments of noise and melody. Where do you think that shit goes?'

He raised a hand to his reddened ear, where a fresh scab crusted the lobe. His finger and thumb pincered into the ear-hole, stretching the skin painfully. The scab popped open. He grunted and extracted a squirming little creature. It was thinner than the worms we collected but still unmistakably one of them – a larva, or a nymph. Half leech, half earthworm. Its round, open mouth blatted out music like a juddering speaker-cone.

'And what if it's not shit at all?' he said, eyes streaming with pain or terror or both. 'What if it's an egg?'

How long has Howard been gone now? A week? A month? I sent a report to the higher-ups about what happened, but nobody from the company seems bothered. They haven't even checked up on me. Just as well; the things run rampant as ever over the glowing clubs and abandoned factories and torn-up roads. Even when the noise of the night subsides, there's always a few hanging about. They sit, supping on the smallest of sounds – the creak of glass in an ill-fitting windowpane, the groan of weeds straining from cracks in the concrete. I know that's what they're eating because I hear these things, too.

I do my best to collect what I can. I crawl on my hands and knees next to the graffitied wall of an unknown club, scraping the things into my bag. A few dozen flee, jumping into drains or wriggling into cracks in the walls. I don't bother with them. There'll always be more to catch.

I wonder how many worms right now must be hatching from their eggs, slithering from sleeping heads. How many are burrowing towards this feeding ground.

I know it's pointless. I don't have the manpower to keep up. Maybe we never did. But I have to try and contain the threat. I have to at the very least undo what has been done to Howard. Before he disappeared, he'd dedicate nearly every waking hour to getting them under control. Now, where he passes the earworms bloom.

Our makeshift evidence room is at the top floor of some abandoned offices. They're going to be demolished soon to make way for a bigger, shinier building. A shame, given all the effort we went to. We soundproofed every inch. Kept each worm caged individually, sealed tight. Maintained a no-talking policy—not even whispers. Fat lot of good it did.

Jars line each wall, stacked from floor to ceiling. The worms lurch and jiggle in their prisons, their mouths puckering around any infinitesimal sound they can grasp. Each one is thinner than when I brought it in and still not a single one has died. The low noise of sticky flesh slipping against glass fills the room.

We tried to destroy them. That was always Plan A. But we can't. Cut them in half, it makes two worms; cut them into a hundred pieces, it makes a hundred. The roar of the incinerator made them grow faster than the flames could consume them. Drowning just made them wet. Howard let me try killing one in every way I could think of, just to show me how impossible it was. So I'd know keeping them locked up, contained, was the only way.

A thousand dark holes slurp in my direction. The sudden roar of a car horn makes me jump. I hear the menacing roar of a trumpet from a nameless Northern Soul song, followed by the repetitive slicing of sampled strings. They're in my head but they've not slithered out. Why haven't they slithered out? Cacophonies unfold inside me. There's no respite now, no intermission. Just constant, endless sound. I raise my hands to my ears, wondering what I might find if I dig around in there.

I can't. I'm not as brave as Howard. Instead, I clap my hands against the sides of my head as hard as I can. There is a sudden crack of white noise and for the briefest moment the songs and snippets and static stop.

Silence. Blissful clarity. A moment I can use. Wheels grind in my head, churning out the silt of a plan.

Howard – what remains of him – goes where the worms are. That has to mean something. Perhaps some part of him is still trying to contain them, even as he's become an agent of their flourishing.

So maybe I don't need to chase him. Maybe I can bring him to me. I march over to where a window should be and tug at the wall of jars. They crash around me and the worms inside convulse in delight. I tear off the foam sound-proofing panels, revealing cardboard plastered in gaffer tape. My nails catch and rip as I claw it away.

Digbeth squats below, muted and silent in the early morning. It's that golden time where the night is over but the birds aren't yet cawing. But it isn't true silence. I've come to understand there's no such thing. The worms flex in their cages, emboldened by the sudden glut of ambient vibration.

My duffel bag slithers like a sack of snakes. I heave it over the sill and drop it out the window. I collect up an armful of jars and throw them out, too. The still morning erupts into breaking glass and barking dogs and the sudden rush of cars. The worms left in the jars fold into themselves, the *O*s of their mouths depressing. They seem afraid. Good.

Half of our evidence lies shattered on the pavement below, the glass strewn across the road like an abstract mosaic. That should be enough. Leaving the remaining jars where they lie, I make my way to the ground floor.

He's already there when I leave the lobby. His overalls writhe, bulging and sucking in around his body. The lo-vis shimmer of the fabric bursts at me in the dawn and I think of fish-scales bristling with light, the silvery plumage of exotic birds. Anything, as long as it's not the sleek sheen of a curling leech.

He'd cut his hair like clockwork, before. Every first Monday of the month. Now, his eyes are half-hidden by the greasy hanks that fall down his forehead. His jaw is buried beneath an uneven beard. What I can see of his face is tight, sunken, hollow.

He opens his mouth and sings in a voice not his own. He's calling me his baby, lamenting our lost love that was never really love anyway.

He turns away from me, hand raised and beckoning. I follow. Stupid and reckless, I know, but what else can I do? I have to hope he'll lead me to the source of this madness. That I'll be able to reverse what's happened to him. To us. I run my nails over my overalls, scratching at the skin beneath. I tell myself nothing is wriggling there, that the itch is just an itch.

The sun sizzles on our skin. Gulls flap their wings above. Distant cars growl and roar. He leads us past The Old Crown and through The Custard Factory, where the last of the night's worms still burrow from the brickwork. Beneath the railway arches, where so many of the things hang like flabby stalactites.

We reach the abandoned boundaries of Digbeth. Empty buildings muscle against one another, broken windows gleaming in the dawn. He crosses the road, arms slack by his sides, and comes to stop outside a disused industrial warehouse. He gestures at me to open the door. I do as he asks. My movements hardly seem my own.

Wet, slithering noises. Creaking wood. Uneven ground, the sound of rocks tumbling down a slope. I squint in the sudden darkness and my eyes adjust in increments to the monstrosity below.

The floor is obliterated, replaced with a yawning maw. In its centre sits a creature whose shape is eminently familiar.

Except it's huge. As big as a house – maybe bigger. Its mouth gapes, dull formless noise pulsing from the hole. Thousands of smaller worms teem around it, worshipping this behemoth, this queen-worm. My head fills with a hissing noise, the sound of my lungs buckling and inflating far too quickly. I tell myself this is impossible even as I know my judgement of such things is long skewed.

Howard steps in line beside me. He no longer smells of deodorant and poorly disguised cigarette smoke. There is a stench of loam and dirt about him, now. The zip on his overalls has come undone. One edge of the fabric flaps down to reveal a mass, undulating. They churn through his skin and clothing like they are tilling soil.

'You're still there,' I say. 'You have to be.' I can't rip my eyes from the mulched gore of his torso. I no longer know who I'm speaking to. 'I don't care about the worms. You can feed and reproduce all you want. Colonise the country if you like. But I want him back.'

'*I want him back.*'

My own voice echoes back at me, mocking. It comes from everywhere – his mouth, the pit, the space between my ears.

He turns to me, his lips moving in a parody of speech. Each word is uttered in a different cadence, a different inflection. A snippet from a news reading; a melodramatic, scripted line from a film; an overheard conversation in a bar; a barked command from a police officer. And beneath it all, a recognisable melody stitching them together.

'If they're in my head, they're in yours too.'

My mind's eye brims with all the long nights spent trawling the streets. The endless complaining and the gossip and the occasional furtive kiss. The slow, exhausted rutting and the microwave ready meals. I didn't love him, no. But there was something there.

He has to come back. There has to be a way, some possibility of reversal. I reach out, try to do his overalls up, give him some semblance of dignity. But the zipper won't close. It catches on something wet, squelching.

His chest is a crumbling cavity. He's gone. We're both gone and it's all our fault.

Worms fall from him, slopping onto the ground. The room fills with music and conversation and writhing wet bodies. And beneath it all is the inhuman noise of a thousand machines whirring and scraping and thunking away, the crashing metallic echoes of dead industry. Industry which began in no small part right here, before anywhere else. I begin to understand why the queen lies nestled in Digbeth, in this graveyard of once thunderous production. Why a century or two ago, she would have claimed this place as her home. Like they all do, she must've followed the sound.

I walk in an aimless daze. They let me go. I suppose I'm not much of a threat. I can't do anything to them except maybe join them. It crossed my mind to ask how long before I become like him. Before my self dissolves, giving way to a slithering din. But I don't want to know. What good would it do?

A homeless man shivers in a doorway. He is coiled in his own arms, knees drawn up his chin. Black rings frame his eyes and his jaw chatters against itself, teeth against teeth like the clack of porcelain plates. He averts his gaze as I approach. We recognise one another.

'You.' The words dribble tired and slow from his mouth. 'Come to move me again?'

'You're cold,' I say. It isn't a question. I can sense the chill. Feel the wind whisper through me, eddying through my perforations.

I slip from my overalls like an insect moulting its shell. Pass him the glimmering clump of fabric that once hemmed me in. His face blanches. He can't take his eyes from the wreckage of my body.

I don't bother looking down at myself. No point. Around me, the city awakens, all rushing vehicles and pounding construction and sliding shutters. Innumerable songs twist their way through my head and I try to focus on the happy ones.

Body Count

KIRSTEN HANDLEY

Lucy's feet continued to pound the tarmac next to Digbeth Branch Canal, every excruciating contact more painful than the last. As part of the marketing team for the upcoming Commonwealth Games, she had designed a poster that assuredly stated running got easier, but she was yet to notice. Her fight with hunger pangs was ongoing and even the unfortunately named Custard Factory building, which she had passed, seemed to taunt her. She pulled the threads of her woollen bracelet as a distraction, desperate to focus on anything but the miserable emptiness in her stomach.

Early morning was Lucy's favourite time of the day. As the sun rose over the canal and the birds erupted into their melodic chorus, it felt like an escape from the long dark nights since moving from Manchester. Wildlife seemed to be the only thing on the planet that was not repulsed by her and whilst she was expecting to see animals of the human variety amongst Digbeth's urban sprawl, she had been pleasantly surprised by its ecosystem. Lucy thought that she saw an otter and as she realised that it was just a log, she careered into a man, which sent her sprawling to the ground.

'I'm so sorry,' a voice said. 'I was in my own little world. Are you hurt?'

Lucy peered upwards to a friendly but somewhat concerned face. Her wrists stung due to slamming them down to protect herself but her legs had been in constant pain since she had started this running regime, so the difference was unnoticeable. As she stared, she realised he was waiting for an answer.

'I'm OK, I'm fine,' she responded in a little voice.

A long arm snaked out and pulled her back onto her feet.

'I'm terrible for being a dreamer and not watching where I'm going,' he said, in a lilt she could not place.

'It's cool, I'm sorry,' Lucy apologised – it was her fault, like everything else.

'Look, you're bleeding,' he said with concern, and she could see he was looking at her wrist. To her relief it was the one without the bracelet wrapped around it.

'I tell you what, let me give you two for one. I'll get you a plaster and a coffee to say sorry,' the man said with a broad grin.

Lucy looked at him anxiously: she still had one mile to go to hit her daily mileage target.

'You really don't have to. Honestly,' she retorted.

'I insist, I don't want you to die of blood poisoning,' he said

Her face turned white.

'I mean not that you will, nothing a hit of caffeine can't fix. I'm Remi, by the way,' he said, holding out a hand.

Remi was a good conversationalist but, more surprisingly, a fantastic tour guide. He did not just wander the streets of Digbeth – he seemed to live them, and his energy pulled her in like nothing else since she had arrived. He laughed when she asked where he was from, before realising his Birmingham accent was alien to her. She panicked when they went into a café at The Custard Factory, before realising it involved black coffee and not sponge pudding.

Remi stuck a plaster on her wrist and she relished her first human interaction since turning up bedraggled at Digbeth coach station, with nothing to show for her life but two sad holdalls. Lucy drank her coffee slowly, trying not to think about the calories it contained.

Once done, they stepped outside and Remi said, 'Well, it was great to knock you over, Lucy Morgan, but some of us have to get to work.'

'What do you do?' she blurted out and kicked herself for being nosy.

'I work in MI5' he whispered as he surveyed the landscape with an expert eye. 'I keep the unruly Digbeth proletariat at bay from the country folk but don't tell anyone.' He put a finger to his lips.

Lucy looked shocked, 'Really?'

He began to laugh, a deep contagious sound that brought warmth to the cold March morning. 'Nah, I work as an estate agent' he said, through a fit of giggles.

Turning, Remi strode off down the canal, whilst Lucy, feeling somewhat idiotic, willed her legs to find that last ounce of energy.

It was a week later and Lucy's feet were burning. Her only human company since meeting Remi had been through pixelated figures on a screen and her negative thoughts, left with no social company, were having an extravaganza.

Her bracelet felt tighter around her wrist.

She must have put on even more weight.

She had looked for Remi every day but this morning he was there once again, ambling down the canal, with black messy hair flopping over his face and a battered satchel thrown on a shoulder.

'Lucy Morgan. At least you managed to stay upright this time and not throw yourself at my feet,' he smirked.

Lucy rolled her eyes at him and kicked herself for the over familiarity. They meandered for a while until he asked: 'Are you a plane spotter?'

She let out a little shriek. 'What, no, why?'

'Ah, you always seem to be looking up, to be fair. Or down, actually. Maybe you're expecting them to crash,' he teased.

Her cheeks turned scarlet and she cursed herself. Last time she had kept up a good pretence of being normal and now that mask was peeling away.

'I like wildlife, you didn't see much where I lived before,' she blurted out, almost as if it was a dark confession.

'A real-life David Attenborough,' Remi said teasing her again. 'I tell you what, I want to hear all about it, whilst you help me pick out a vintage sofa.'

'A sofa?' She looked doubtful – she knew she was weird but she was not used to human beings who bought furniture on a whim with acquaintances they barely knew.

'Yeah, I have to dress this incredible loft apartment and my mate who runs an antique shop lets me borrow things for a very short while,' Remi said and he linked his arm through hers, leading the way.

Lucy told Remi that she was unlikely to be helpful, her experience of furniture having been limited to watching other people assemble flatpack, screaming for various screws and spanners to be passed over.

'You're talented creatively though, right? You do graphics. I'm not bringing you to build one,' Remi said, his hand brushing against hers.

Lucy felt confused: it was just her job.

They wandered around the shop until she stopped in front of a lemon-yellow sofa, its warmth providing a tonic to the greyness of the day.

'It's a bit bright, Luce,' he said.

She smiled despite herself. It had been a long time since anyone had called her that and she almost forgot to curse that she had picked incorrectly.

'It reminds me of one of my favourite birds, a goldfinch. I saw one the other day' she blurted out. She realised how stupid that sounded.

'Ah, my boss will love that, let's go for it,' he said, jumping on its seat. 'Flats around here have a reputation for being less boujee than those around the Mailbox or Brindley Place but I'm on a mission to prove people wrong.'

The two place names meant nothing to Lucy but she suddenly felt some pride in her tiny one-bedroom studio. At least it had the right postcode.

Remi exalted Lucy's interior design capabilities to his mate as they chatted through the practicalities of the loan. When they exited, Remi asked Lucy for her phone number and she winced. Her phone still provided an uncomfortable portal to the past but she nervously read out the digits to him, then declined his offer to join a group of friends for a burger that evening.

A week later and the blister on the back of Lucy's heel was making her run even more nightmarish than usual – tears were rolling down her cheeks – yet she forced herself to keep going, continually pulling her bracelet even tighter. She had arranged to meet Remi later in the morning but to her dismay he was early.

'Are you alright Luce? You don't look the best,' he said, concern apparent in his voice.

'It's just allergies,' she said, in a voice that was not her own.

Remi went to say something but stopped himself. 'How about we find a bench? I bought you something.'

They sat down and even though she had made no reference to it, he pulled a box of plasters out of his satchel and stuck one on her heel, pretending to be a lifesaving surgeon. He rummaged in his bag further and pulled out a clumsily wrapped parcel in brown paper with a red bow. Lucy pinched her bracelet to her wrist almost cutting the circulation: surprises were dark monsters that attacked unexpectedly.

She tore the paper open gently, being careful to override her tendency to be too impulsive.

'Ah rip it, Luce,' Remi said. 'My wrapping is horrendous anyway.'

With one determined tear she pulled apart the paper, wondering which shadowy figure was going to jump out. But she was presented with a large wildlife book.

'One of my mates took the photos around here but it's still pretty cool and I thought you'd like it,' Remi said, beaming at her.

For a second, as she threw her arms around him, her blister pain was replaced by joy.

Two days later and Lucy and Remi were bird watching down the canal, trying to match the species with the images captured in the book. A handwritten sheet of paper fell out of its pages and hurriedly she went to retrieve it but she could not stop Remi seeing the strict target numbers, underlined in red pen. A shadow crossed his face and he paused for a second but Lucy could not unlock the tight padlock of her secrets and she stayed quiet. His next retort was to make a joke about why the seagulls visited so far from home and relief flooded her body.

It was the weekend and Lucy had been invited by Remi to a bar which specialised in indoor curling. She'd called the venue beforehand to check that the curling pitch was away from the pungent smells coming from the kitchen and had turned up late, in order to avoid participating in the excruciating ritual of dinner. Whilst her pint of lime and soda water looked out of place next to four frothy beers, none of the other friends he had invited commented on it.

'I'm rubbish at curling,' Lucy said, as she sent her first attempt far away from the target. This had disaster written all over it: a public show of her inadequacy and the chance to loosen the only thread of connection she had in this city.

Her lack of talent confining herself to her studio flat.

No company but little ants that ran down her window.

Everyone else thinking she was a disgusting failure.

'Ah you've done better than me, Luce,' Remi said, putting his arm around her shoulder. 'Not like we do this every weekend.'

The arm felt comforting and she willed him not to move but he soon let go and ambled up for his turn.

To Lucy's surprise, she improved at curling and whilst she said very little, simply smiling as Remi and his friends fiercely debated the recent Digbeth construction project, she wondered whether these people may genuinely like her.

Three weeks later and the smell inside the cake baking experience tent was making Lucy nauseous. Baking did not mean eating, she repeated almost as a mantra but the excess of chocolate, icing and sugar was a sensory disaster. She had wanted to cherish the extended time with Remi, only the walls were closing in, trapping her inside. Lucy tried to focus on the mallard they had seen flying down the canal but her own flight response was being activated, driven by panic. Lucy careered outside throwing up violently, as Remi held back her hair.

Being sick provoked a contradictory mix of revulsion and relief but the shame that *he* had seen it caused tears to fall down her cheeks.

'I'm so sorry,' she said, through sobs.

'It's OK, Luce.' He rubbed her back gently, making delicate circles. 'I shouldn't have made you do that, I didn't think.'

'It's not your fault,' Lucy said, tears filling her eyes, voice rising in anguish, 'it's mine. I'm sorry. I'm a mess. I ruin everything.'

Remi looked sad.

Whilst Lucy had thought the disaster of baking would mean that Remi wanted nothing more to do with her, they met for coffee every day. He focused on giving her a history lesson, describing the ghosts of souls that walked the streets of Digbeth and the dilemma of how to embrace the future whilst respecting their legacy.

Both Remi and Lucy wanted to ask questions of each other but did not know how to start so they stayed within the safety of Digbeth's regeneration.

It was Friday night and they sat in a boardgames café. Lucy decided it was now or never and placed a hand on his cheek. Emboldened by the fact he did not move it away, she brushed her lips against his.

'Wait, no, Luce,' Remi said, pushing her away.

Her body froze for a second, realising the sheer magnitude of his gesture.

Another human had adjudicated on her existence and rejected it. Her mind flashed back to the painful similarities of leaving Manchester.

She snatched her handbag and ran out, her speed elevated by months of training.

Two months later and Lucy was running down the canals for longer now but it required getting up earlier to ensure avoiding Remi. Her calorie count was more restrictive because the Commonwealth Games were over and she had taken on a new graphics role for a fitness wear brand. During her interview she had thought they would laugh her out the building and tell her to apply to Cadbury's. She was puzzled when they offered her the job but now faced the new challenge of severe imposter syndrome.

'Lucy,' said a voice she recognised.

She refused to look back but Remi frustratingly kept up with her, in a marked contrast to his usual languid stroll.

'Please slow down, Luce, I'm not as fit as you, I can't do it,' he said, wheezing.

'You're not interested, so leave me alone,' she said, cringing at how pathetic her voice sounded.

'It's not that. It just would be wrong, or at least it would be wrong right now,' he said, panting.

Reluctantly, Lucy stopped for a second – the lack of food was making her brain fuzzy and trying to do two things was tipping it over the edge.

'Why make all this effort with me?' she said, angry at both the interruption to her routine and the reminder of her shortcomings.

'Look, I'll be honest. To start with, I saw you on the floor and you just looked so sad and lost,' he responded whilst he grabbed his hip, fighting an oncoming stitch.

'So you felt sorry for me,' she said, cross now.

'Yes. I mean no, but then I got to know you and found out you're cool. I'm not explaining myself well, but I just want to be your friend. You make me feel good and I want to make you feel good. I want to help you get better. Let me help you chuck everything you think you know about yourself in the canal. Right in there, along with all the other trash that nobody ever wants to resurface. Sorry, that's an awful metaphor but you get me,' he said.

Lucy was silent and pulled at her bracelet. It snapped off. She let out an anguished cry. 'I just hate…'

Lucy got to her knees to retrieve the scraps of wool from the floor. It gave her an excuse not to finish her sentence.

'Hate what?' Remi said.

'Me.'

And then Lucy stuttered and willed herself to stop. Yet the negative words would not comply and tumbled out like a swarm of bees as she described her painful final days in Manchester. Remi let her finish and then pulled Lucy into a hug and she cried until she was empty.

Three months later and Lucy met Remi for a walk down the canal. Remi was pointing excitedly at the water, jabbing his finger. Lucy looked down to see a furry face, with long whiskers – it was definitely not a log. She touched her wrist but the bracelet had long gone and as she looked at the otter, she realised that what she was feeling was something like hope.

You Can Go Home Again

TAYLOR BURNS

Digbeth, December, stars in the sky like someone had shook out a rug-full of them.

He was back in Brum, home for the first time in a decade, ambling around a city he misremembered – buds wedged in his ears, a small slim paperback with a sun-buckled spine blooming from his back pocket.

In his hand, a mini Moleskine with an address sticker across the front cover. It says, in lilting black Sharpie, *Lines*. This was where he wrote his best metaphors, similes, words to use later, most recent of which was *Reliquary*, a shrine for holy artefacts. Before that, written above a fleuron he'd drawn to distinguish *Words of Note* and *Possible Lines* for later use, it read: *[like] mussels on a rope*.

He wrote that a few weeks ago, when he was still living elsewhere, recently dumped (and depressed before that anyway), looking for a phrase that might best describe the pain that was grimly clinging to him.

Now he plans to write new notes in it, observations on the topography of home, witty dicta about Birmingham and its buildings and its spaces and its people. He's even bought a special pencil, a whole box of them, striking cedar-wood Blackwings, £36 for twelve. Steinbeck used them when he wrote *East of Eden*. It was time to get serious like that. Never mind that he was skint; you couldn't put a price on what he planned to write now that he was home: breathless page-long paragraphs for later insertion into his novel, his prose a long string of pearl; gorgeous free verse about random residents, short devastating arias, descriptions of people *back home* that were bleak but always tuneful.

It's true that he didn't want to be back in Birmingham. After so long away, down South, where after a decade all his friends and possibilities were — the bulk of his good memories, too — being home felt like failure. It was like the last ten years had been lost, taken off him as if in a video game. He'd lost his partner of nine years — and by extension their flat and then his job — the whole span of his twenties whipped away from him, the reveal of which cracked in the air like a toreador's cloth. But, like, if he could just get some graft out of it, come back and write something true, not the mimeographed short fiction he'd been pissing about with, his own versions of stuff by dead American giants, but something radical, real, desperate, lived. If he could get even one story cycle out of it, one immortal poem, fatless, smooth, like a seawall, like a river stone. If he could just write one thing born in Brum to cut through the all the bullshit in his brain, laid there by being regretfully and terminally online, and all the bollocks he'd experienced on the Scene — he'd been trying for two years to get a literary agent, a process that had flushed all the hope his talent had instilled out of him, like a beer-line being cleaned — if he could just write one serious thing, something that told him about himself, or told people like him something honest about their own lives, then the fact that the only world he'd known since he was twenty had just had its history wiped — like someone had clicked the little [x] in the corner of his life — it might all well be worth it.

(*Must cut the technological lexicon,* he wrote, *move the chains, write in rust and iron about steel and archways, factories surrounded by moats of silt muddied wet-orange with rain…*)

His work, or rather his research, the reconnaissance of his past, for so long pushed down to a hadal place within him, started in Bournville, where his father died when his son was twelve, in a house given to him by the village trust on account of his cancer, which had spread from leg to lung.

Later he found him, dead on his bed, called the ambulance himself, knocked for the neighbour and told him through a scream what had happened.

On the few times he'd been back to Birmingham over the years he took a trip to his dad's, so close to Cadbury World that sometimes as a child he would run to the corner and catch chocolate on the air.

Those times he had walked past the house only on the opposite side of the road, the odd-numbered side. He would glance up when he was in line with it and then carry on to *The Country Girl* at the end of the street before going back four fags later a different way.

This time, though, he was going to walk right past it, stop if it was coast clear, sneak a picture, trail his hand along the black wooden bannister as he moved off, like a kid playing a stick across palisade fencing.

When he got there a man was edging the lawn with a fruit-bright orange strimmer, grass flecks falling on the path behind him. In the porch, his son was sitting in an egg of light let in by a glassless window, watching him in shorts and boots and shin pads. When he explained that he used to live there and asked if he could take a picture of the old place, the bloke invited him into the garden. His wife was pruning a rose bush that had not been planted when he lived there. He spent the next twenty minutes small-talking about his father's house, dropping so nonchalantly into conversation that his dad had died in what was now the couples' bedroom that he shocked himself — talking about it out loud to his closest friends or even his family was previously unachievable; he'd lock up like an old steering wheel.

This was the progress he was making, then — in *The Country Girl* he wrote an hour's worth of notes in a wild doctor's hand, chicken scratch about his father's garden, where he'd once sat on a little wall of wooden border roll while he waited for help and where there were still four holes drilled into the brickwork from when dad put up a backboard the summer he got into basketball — and after Bournville he went round Weoley Castle, where he lived with his mom and sister afterwards, before planning to move on to King's Heath, Quinton, The Jewellery Quarter, any town the train would take him — Gosta Green, Yardley, Queslett — a place a week, so that by mid-March his Moleskine might be a deep well of lines and notes, addenda, errata, pages of dashed-off ornery driftwood that might later be broken up and sanded down into something special.

Digbeth, though, and the pencil lies unsharpened in his pocket. His Moleskine is out, crippling in the wind. But it's not open merely a rest, a music stand for his phone, which he keeps out, clutched to the notepad's cover with a cold thumb.

They have been texting every three minutes for seventeen hours a day.

It started the night after his father's garden — a story he told within an hour of knowing Clara, hoping it would distinguish him from your usual dating-app dickhead — and has continued since and won't ever stop because tonight in Digbeth he just knows.

Knows because all around him is what he wanted, needed; the material he'd been missing. He had got the personal stuff, quarried that from Bournville, where a Quaker sensibility still held, hushed in the air like a minute's silence. Next, it was the city, the non-London scaffolding to his story. And here it was, all around him, above him, Birmingham, blue-collar, as English as a brick but polished now with a slight glint of dew. And still he didn't write a word.

It had been six days; his screen time was absurd; his eyes overexposed to blipping bluelight, injurious. He texted her on the seventh morning, said he wouldn't be about as much today, he was gonna rewater his eyes, perform a digital detox by checking out Digbeth, one of the few areas of mainland Brum he didn't really have a memory from, save maybe the time he went up there one weekend with his home mates, not long before he left for university back in twenty-ten.

Back then, they were versed on Broad Street, the boys. To a lad they were nineteen and underfed, looked like lemons in baggy jeans and hand-me-down smart shoes and wide-cuffed dress shirts ironed to a snap like flags. For some reason, a few of them wore plastic rosary beads around their necks, Day-Glo ones that lit up ghostly in nightclub pictures. They tried Digbeth one night, for a change. Stood in a queue for a club under a rattling bridge, where suddenly they seemed square. They waited for ten more minutes before someone said, Shall we sack it in?

A mate who had moved back recently said Digbeth was the one, now, though, and probably always had been.

He wanted to see for himself, told Clara he wouldn't be on WhatsApp much, an unthinkable thing, a dreaded admission for a pair who in six days over the phone and FaceTime (Clara was away for Christmas) had shared stories of dead dads and heart attack mothers, siblings they felt unmoored from.

Moreover, they were frankly just too hot for each other, had had to make do so far with pictures and videos, their respective galleries a florilegium of shared smut, the symmetry they felt sexually – both were unashamedly kinky, and met on an app where your bio was meant to be an exegesis on what you desired instead of the usual dreck about the gym or homeowning or the nonpareil benefits of being a dog person – only heightening the desperate need they had to fuck each other arseways.

If he was going to get working again, he'd need to regain his attention, though. Lock his phone off. Swap it for a boxfresh Blackwing. He'd bought a book en route – a supplement to the old Pan edition of an Alan Sillitoe he had in his back pocket – a Pevsner Architectural Guide to the buildings of Birmingham, the only thing he'd be looking at when he paused his tour for turbid pints of inky Guinness, he told her.

Clara agreed it would be good for them, the no phones thing. She was back teaching in the new year, and a day at her desk would help her feel more prepared for the new class of kids she was inheriting at the small SEN school she taught at in Sparkbrook.

Digbeth was doing its thing around him. Evening darkness had set in, the sky a crush of pepper-coloured stars. People were going into pubs, coming out of them. Everywhere smelt cosy, the warming crackle of a winter cigarette. An old bit of building read, in dripping carmine like it had just been spray-canned on, *This Wall Stays*. A graffiti rendition of Theresa May was painted inside an old garage's entranceway and she did indeed look lizardlike. Next door to the coach station the clack of resin on resin sounded out from a bar's pool table, its burgundy felt stained with lakes of spilt drink that showed up black like lung air on an X-ray.

This was all very much his Shit — and he hadn't clocked any of it.

The leftovers of industry were all around him. After a decade down South, in the milieu of academia, universities, even the bar he worked at in the lounge of an exclusive health club in Summertown, an absolute middle-class fever dream of rude Yoga Moms and arrogant Rugby Men, a place that somehow still paid its Food and Beverage Team — which he was a part of while he tried to fund his Masters and who were dragged prey-like around their shifts by a customer base who seemed to pride themselves on how rude they could be to service staff (and also by a hierarchal ecosystem which referred to F&B as *tertiary revenue* and treated its workforce commensurately) — *still* only paid them minimum wage while those in the sales office pulled in £30k for Signing People Up, this despite the fact that their week ended with a half-day and pastries from an *artisanal* bakery and the bar team's ended with them all passing around a pot of chartreuse-green O'Keeffe's hand repair, the only thing that helped soothe the palms and knuckles following a kitchen shift, after a decade of that, this was exactly where he wanted to be, back home, among his people, the accent everywhere amid the bustle of a smoky winter's evening.

But beneath the dribbling arches, opposite an abandoned shunt line, he was lost in the space age of his phone. The book he bought went untouched save for the picture he sent her, which had the Moleskine assembled squarely on top and said: *Your replacements for the night*. He dared not close his apps for fear of losing her, though — ever since Dad his tendency had been toward catastrophe, apocalypse — and because of this instant dart towards disaster he knew that he loved her already, quite badly, to the point that the love now was interweaved inevitably with dying. When for instance she blue-ticked him that night for twenty minutes while she made tea, his thoughts warped like they did in the weeks after his father's death, when his mother left him playing with a neighbour so that she could do the big shop she hadn't been able to do since her son found his father curled like a comma on his bed. She said she'd be an hour, maybe two. She took three, the last hour of which he spent convincing himself she was boiling in flames in her once-blue Mercedes Sprinter, somewhere just off the Bristol Road. And then someone would come and tell him and take him away.

It all became too much. He tapped away at Uber, asked them to come get him. He'd return to look properly at Digbeth soon, when his already nervous infrastructure wasn't newly on fire with the seismograph of wait-breathe-wait that was chatting up someone new and potentially perfect.

It hadn't previously felt like this, in the week that they'd been talking. Real life hadn't existed thus far for him and Clara, who had spent the entire timeframe of their relationship texting and calling from the sanctum of their bedrooms – it was their rules and their world, gifted to them by a Christmas break which helixed together their time. But something hit him now, then. Clara was a teacher, prepping her classes. He was back in Brum, a little bit lost, thin, intense, jobless, thirty; his only plan was to write his way out of it, even if he didn't know what *it* was, exactly. All of a sudden it became clear that this could fade away, go down as the time he was given a brief bit of hope upon moving home before it was taken from him by the dream-crushing drudgery of just... living. He didn't even get half a Guinness.

A week later he was back in town, Clara in tow, looping his arm as they lapped the central roadworks en route to the Custard

Factory. They'd had one date already, under a canopy of fairy lights in a Harborne beer garden, a thick blanket over their lap. Beneath it, an ampersand of knee and hip, his and hers twisted together while he ate her neck and the waitress coughed awkwardly to get their attention as a carafe of red clinked against a par of web-thin wine glasses in the centre of a wobbling tray.

Date two was Digbeth.

He was keen to show off his credentials as a cool and pensive kid after so long withholding his taste and core beliefs from anywhere that wasn't a classroom. And, as in Longbridge, where he was living and where a commissioned sign at the end of his road said *I Slept to the Sound of Hammers*, he felt an affinity with the artistic possibilities of the place, wanted Clara to be a part of his newfound confidence when it came to confessing what it was he believed in.

Despite this, they ended up in a sports bar showing the boxing because it was Saturday night and they hadn't booked anywhere.

But never mind. In the corner, by a frost-dappled single-pane window, they dragged together a couple of chairs, folded into each other again, kissed, made promises, said, This is mad, ennit?

A shmaltzy cheap-seat song came over the speakers, intermingled with the ringside commentary, and took on the importance of high and lustrous art as they said I Love You in stupid harmony.

Walking to the station he stopped her under an archway, pushed her hips flush to the damp brick, dipped his hand into her jeans, wrapped his fist around the delicate lacework of her underwear as her eyes exploded a flickering black. A couple came round the corner, hurrying them into a giggling let's-go.

He put her on the train home at Moor Street, its old-style signage beaded with rain and the Selfridges building looming large above it, a great spaceship slick wet like it had just been birthed there.

He was home.

The Skin Pits

MATTHEW GIDLEY

A fly settles on the tip of her nose, its buzzing and tickling penetrating her sleep, merging with the beating of her heart which she senses in pounding pulses as she twitches once, twice, and jerks awake. She waves a hand in irritation and looks around, squinting, surprised at her surroundings.

Over by the wattle fence which separates the tannery from the boundary ditch, a hen with a milky eye pecks at bristle and fat and sinew, clumps of it in little gluey piles around the pickets. Most days she does not notice the stench, but in August the heat is smothering and it catches in her throat like tar. The hen's eye is the same colour as the liquefying mass of hooves and horn-core glistening in a leather bucket next to the vinegar pit. A smoky yellow jelly alive with flies. She saw a man like that once, at the Ascensiontide fair, a blind man, beating a drum for a dancing bear. He turned his yellow gaze towards her, seemed to see right into her and through her, and she fled. She slept that night in the bean field, afraid to go home in case the man was there.

This was three summers ago.

She still has nightmares.

The dead eye staring into her.

Next to the stretching frames, her brother, not yet six years old and brandishing a wooden pole three times his height, is stirring the contents of the leeching pit – a stinken brown soup of water and stale beer, fermented barley, oak bark and acorns. He stirs slowly, in wide arcs, pressing the skins deeper into the tanning solution, humming, absorbed in his task. She wonders what he is thinking, this gentle strong boy who never talks – does the stink reach him as it does her, do the flies concern him?

His humming reminds her of a dog they had seen, trampled by cattle on the way to market and thrown into the moat. How days later, they had visited the corpse and found it bloated, obscene, bursting with maggots and flies. She had vomited while her brother just stared and hummed, the tune of a song they both loved, a harvest song, about a god in the woods who always comes when you need him, protecting you from danger, scooping you up to save your soul. But there was no god like that really, she knew – it was just a song. The dog was stinking proof.

She shudders at the memory, blinks, looks back across at the willow fence and feels an urge to slip away. It will only be for a while and the boy probably won't even notice. The day is too hot. The river is calling. She leaps the fence and is gone.

A short dash away from the edge of town and into the valley, a marshy place even in midsummer, springy and swampy, riddled with secrets. Tall grass, reeds that tower above her head, things alive in the green which rustle and chirrup as she presses towards her special place. There is an ancient midden here, known only to her, near a bend in the river where the water slows into a broad, shallow pool. A mound of potsherds and splinters of fired clay, fragments of orange and red glaze that reflect the sunlight, dazzling her eyes. There are greys and browns and whites too, hints of pattern, all jumbled together in a hill of forms and edges which skitter and settle pleasingly beneath her feet as she scrambles to its summit.

Across the river, spindles of smoke rise from Deritend smithies and merge into clouds that hang like gauze above the valley. A distant clanking of hammers is carried on the breeze. The reeds are whispering. The sun in her eyes makes dots and colours.

She feels drowsy and alive, connected to everything, connected to nothing.

A bell tinkles – far away, now much nearer – and a prickle of goosebumps tells her that she is no longer alone. Turning her head to watch a damselfly settle on a reed, she freezes.

A little round man in a crimson jacket squats next to her on the midden, a gold bell on his hat, his face dark with fury. He yanks a crystal orb from his pocket and thrusts it before her face.

'Lok!' he screeches, snapping at her with tiny pointed teeth, tapping on the crystal with claw-like fingernails.

She stares, terrified, as the orb's inner light flashes and swirls, clearing to reveal an image that makes her cry out: the boy, her brother, floating face down in the leeching pit.

The man grabs her wrist and shouts 'Yow ydel mayde! Sluggard! Sitteth doun whil that thi brother werketh!'

She stands, slides, begins to run but he pulls her back, his rage softening to a kind of sadness. 'He is on lif,' he murmurs, 'Lob hath maked hym sauf. Alle is wel.'

He places a hand over his heart and bows his head as if in prayer. She sees the wetness, the brown stains on the sleeves of his soaking jacket and she understands that the boy is safe. When he looks at her again, the man's eyes are shining with tears. 'Thou shuldest have hadden mo care!' he tells her, then repeats the words more slowly, wagging his finger with each syllable.

She closes her eyes and nods and when she opens them again, he is gone, the jingling of his bell receding among the reeds. She stands, turns and the boy is there, running towards her, stumbling through the tall grass, drenched, filthy. His hair is matted, eyes stinging red, face contorted in grief. He screams but makes no sound. She holds out her hands, reaching for him, touching, drawing him towards her. He burrows into her embrace and she feels the life surging within him. They rock together, gently, flesh and blood, skin on skin, until his breathing slows and he begins to hum.

Glamour

KAREN ARNOLD

Crowded in front of the tiny mirror for hours before we emerge. Music to get us in the mood. We all have different preferences. Cally remembers traditional Irish songs, singing along as she curls her hair. I tell her that she sounds like a banshee wailing. She replies that the Bean Si is a good friend of hers and she'll thank me not to be rude. Morena plays haunting violin music that has wolves in the wires and carries the scent of snow and pine forest. My taste is for metal, the sound born from the factories and foundries, the roar that moves through my veins.

Dark kohled eyes, deep red lips, the whitest teeth. Gold flashes in our ear lobes, at our throat. Plumes of glamour wreath around us, an incense of perfume and hairspray, the result of all our ancient skill and craft, we are poised to take our place on the Saturday night stage that is the High Street, among the crowds that spill out of The Institute

Joyous, shimmering with anticipation, running soft, jewelled hands over slim hips, pushing our fingers through Salome shining hair, we are ready to dance. In the blink of an eye, we stand at the edge of the city night ocean. Neon stars and a tide of humanity running high under a full moon

Arm in arm, we abandon ourselves to the night, to the foaming, fizzing froth of it. Music pours from the darkness of open doors. The hot summer night is suddenly split by the blue edge of a siren and like eels slipping through the darkness of the

Sargasso, over wet fields, into the oil black cut, instinct tells us what to do, when to hunt alone. Without words we select our victims, calling them with smoky eyes and fluid hips, perfumed skin and parted lips. Whispers and kisses in the silence below the drum and bass, deeper and deeper.

In the delicate dawn light, we move silently, arm in arm through streets gleaming with the detritus of pleasure. Propitiatory shrines made of half-full wine bottles, empty beer glasses, one abandoned silver stiletto. A mallard and his wife glide through the canal basin on water turned into a ribbon of burnished steel by the rising sun. He nods respectfully as we pass each other. We drift back to our lair among the arches.

When they wake alone, feeling that they have aged ten years after the best night of their lives — well, my sisters and I agree, fair exchange is no robbery.

From Whitlock's End

JOSH ALLEN

Earlyish, on a sunny morning about Easter time, I set out by train from Moor Street Station in the heart of Birmingham to Whitlock's End, right on the edge of the city.

The morning's objective is to walk around 8 miles back to Digbeth. The twist being that I will walk almost the entire way along waterways. Two canals, one brook and a river, to be precise.

Almost uniquely amongst Britain's major cities, we do not associate Birmingham with a major river. The eddies, flows and surges that residents and outsiders alike associate the city with are those of traffic. If we think about Birmingham and waterways at all, it is in the context of the city's location at the heart of the canal network. It was these artificial waterways, mostly dug over the course of two generations in the final third of the 18th and first third of the 19th Century, which enabled Birmingham's growth from a scrappy north Warwickshire market town to one of the greatest metropolises in Atlantic Europe. Ingenious engineering provided a constant and consistent level of water to the canals, making the bulk transport of goods regularised and predictable for the first time ever.

This said, Birmingham's fate and trajectory has been tied to water and waterways for far longer than most people imagine. Much as Manchester's development was shaped by the Irwell, Leeds the Aire and Sheffield the Don, so Birmingham has been formed by its myriad of little rivers, brooks and streams.

Whitlock's End is one of the most northerly settlements in Worcestershire. It is a suburban dormitory community, with the aesthetic of one hundred years of car-centred ribbon and infill development to match. Though it is the kind of place where the few daytime pedestrians cheerily greet you as you pass, these days it is overshadowed by its neighbour Dickens Heath, a post-modern mini new town, just over the border in the Metropolitan Borough of Solihull. Whitlock's End, however, got here first, so the little park and ride station on the Birmingham to Stratford-upon-Avon railway line bears its name.

Of particular significance on this walk, Whitlock's End is situated very close to the watershed between the drainage basins of the River Severn and the River Trent.

To the south and west stretches the Severn basin. The countryside is gently hilly, often wooded, highly agricultural and rural, where the trees have been felled. It has its large towns, small cities, metal sheds and suburban tracts like anywhere but nowhere are you far from the traditional countryside. It is a land of Morris Dancers, part-timbered buildings, ancient earthworks, green lanes, 12th Century churches, hop rows and cider orchards.

The Green Man, Pan, Penda, myths and legends.

Extending north and east, encompassing most of central England including Birmingham and the wider West Midlands county, is the River Trent's basin. This land also has its myths of legends: *Sir Gawain and the Green Knight* was probably written by a medieval clerk from somewhere near Stoke-on-Trent. They took their inspiration from the craggy, creviced limestone dales and bleak plateaus of the Peak District. However, in the main the Trent basin is a bastion of industrial and post-industrial England. Pockmarked by former collieries and industrial sites, redeveloped as warehouses, retail parks and Barrett houses, its ring roads link the surviving factories with office parks and garden centres. The mighty River Trent, heavily canalised, has narrowboats bobbing up and down on it. Its banks house a couple of coal-fired power stations, still belching out their plumes of steam while generating the power for iPads, smartwatches, Teslas and all the other gizmos of the 2020s.

But not for much longer – the days of these mid-20th Century dragons are numbered.

For me, the fact that Birmingham has developed just north of this topographical dividing line between the North and the South Midlands is crucial for understanding its character. Just as its location belies, Birmingham is a complex mixture and agglomeration of the rural counties to its south-west and the industrialised-cum-post-industrial region to its north-east, which culturally and historically has a lot in common with Northern England.

The first waterway I follow back into Birmingham is testimony to the city's pivotal role as a bridge between north and south. Opened at the dawn of the 19th Century, the Stratford-upon-Avon Canal meanders south from King's Norton, in Birmingham's southernmost reaches. Today it is a peaceful and tranquil backwater, a haven for wildlife and all manner of gongoozlers. When it opened, it was intended as a quick way of linking up Birmingham and London. It even carried coal hewn near Dudley, via the ill-fated Lapal Tunnel, destined for combustion in the Great Wren.

On the morning I walk the route, I slip through a small patch of greenbelt out of Worcestershire, across a slither of Solihull and through estates of modern semi-detached homes, constructed in the last 40 odd years.

The towpath is quiet. A middle-aged woman, her bike laden with panniers, overtakes me and stops a little further up the path. She takes out her phone and snaps a few frames. Seeing me, she calls back, 'I hope you don't mind, it is such a lovely morning I just had to take some photos to send my friend.'

'Not at all,' I respond, 'it is a lovely day for it.'

Sliding through more housing estates and little clusters of greenery, the canal enters Birmingham – an arrival heralded by the sight of a National Express West Midlands single decker gliding over a squat concrete road bridge, a little further up the tree lined cut.

After the bridge, it is time to turn off, making for the nearby line of the Chinn Brook, my second waterway of the day.

I follow the distant figure of a young man wearing a large olive coat into a woodland nature reserve. Presently, I hear a hacking cough echo through the trees. It is the man I've just glimpsed, sat on a bench, clutching a massive roll-up, spluttering away.

Instinctively I say 'Bless you,' as I pass him.

Still trying not to cough, he says, 'Thanks, mate. I only got out of the hospital about an hour ago.' He holds up an impressively bandaged hand and waves the equally impressive joint. 'Still, I managed to roll myself this blunt.'

'Nicely done!' I congratulate him. 'Hope you have a better rest of the day!'

All uncharacteristically chatty for the edge of Birmingham. Must be the spring sunshine. First the cyclist and keen social photographer, now this unfortunate chap consoling himself with a mid-morning spliff in a suburban woodland nature reserve.

Soon I reach the Chinn Brook. I follow it along its bank, down a kind of green corridor. This eventually turns into a long, thin, sloping recreation ground, busy with people out strolling – alone or in groups – or walking their dogs.

Billesley was first developed as a council estate in the 1920s and 1930s, as Birmingham expanded into this once sparsely populated rural chunk of northern Worcestershire. The council's architects, engineers and planners left strips of open ground like this, partly to create communal space for the new residents leaving the old neighbourhoods of the inner city behind, partly out of necessity to allow rainfall runoff and mitigate against the Chinn Brook flooding.

The result is that almost a quarter of Birmingham is still green space, kept fertile by the city's countless little waterways.

These large tracts of open, wild areas are unrivalled in other large cities and, personally, I have always found this understated, quietly pleasant quality of Birmingham far more attractive than the tourism office's oft – repeated bombast that the city has 'more miles of canals than Venice.'

Further along the Chinn Brook, I reach rows of prefabs, almost unique, some still inhabited but all testament to the emergency housing constructed in the thousands to home bomb damage victims, during and immediately after World War II.

The Chinn Brook now merges with the River Cole, its waters intermixing with those of the more substantial stream to continue the passage northwards, up through Birmingham and eventually out along the River Trent and into the North Sea.

The River Cole runs through Hall Green and the wooded land beside the stream would have drawn Constable's eye, had he been a Brummie. The course of the waterway, almost fantastical, feels far removed from the busy city around it.

Appropriately enough, I soon emerge onto the side of the road opposite Sarehole Mill. Famously, the mill has been suggested as the model for the watermill near Hobbiton in J.R.R. Tolkein's Middle Earth novels. He grew up nearby, in the years immediately prior to World War I.

These days, as a rare surviving, near-intact example of a watermill, Sarehole Mill is run as a museum by Birmingham Museums Trust. Its history is a fascinating encapsulation of how watermills and waterpower led to the development of industry in Birmingham. Birmingham's larger rivers like the Cole, the Tame, the Rea and the Bournbrook provided motive power for medieval and early modern industry on a small scale, long before steam power entered the frame. Sarehole Mill was no different. Prior to his world-changing partnership with the Scottish scientist and engineer James Watt, Matthew Boulton, the factory owner and money man of the infamous duo, leased Sarehole Mill in the 1750s and 1760s and set it to rolling metal. A typical example of the interchangeable, jobbing uses of these early factories.

Shortly after Sarehole Mill, I pass one of my favourite features on the walk. Approaching a seemingly normal suburban road, I spy off to the right, a ford. Not a car of a make commonly encountered in suburban south Birmingham, rather a place where the road slopes gently down towards the River Cole and instead of there being a bridge, vehicles drive straight through the water.

Not long after my walk, I mention this quite in passing to a trade union comrade and she reminisces about playing there, decades before, as a small child. She says at the time, it felt like the beach. And why ever not? One of my pet theories is that being starved of a coastline, Midland people will quite happily make anywhere with water the seaside.

A little way further on and perched in the middle of the stream are a flight of concrete stepping stones — another fun touch, adding to the interest of the walk.

This section along the River Cole is called The Shire Country Park. A knowing nod to local boy J.R.R. Tolkien and there is certainly something otherworldly about encountering a ford and stepping stones just a few miles from the centre of Britain's second largest city.

By now, when I glimpse the housing on either side of the stream, its character is changing. The 1930s semis and low-rise modernist flats of the inner suburbs giving way to older, more unabashedly urban Victorian terraces.

Soon I burst into a little park beside the Stratford Road in Springfield. Here on my left, a squat but imposing brick-built early 20th Century church has been converted into a South Asian restaurant. A creative adaptation of an existing local building as the needs of the community change.

To my right a weathered but still immensely sturdy red brick bridge, constructed by Birmingham Corporation in 1914, still performing its function of carrying road traffic to and from the city centre.

Continuing along the River Cole beyond Stratford Road, the waterway's green character remains undiminished, even as the backs of warehouses and little factory units loom close to it – backs often broken up by the occasional scrap of well-used allotment land.

Passing through a gap between two terraced houses, I enter a nature reserve on the site of a former brickworks. The reserve is unkempt and verdant, populated by Ash and similar trees, which are often found growing on discarded industrial sites. By contrast, the other side of the river is a near solid wall of factories, depots and warehouses. A reminder that the manufacture and distribution of goods remain as much a part of Birmingham's present and likely future as its past.

Leaving the former brickworks behind, I am somewhat discombobulated to cross the campus-like business park of a major engineering services firm, aeons away from the small workshops and lockups surrounding it. At the entrance to this site stands a 1950s vintage navy jet, preserved and placed on a post. It's clearly a celebration of the quiet but pivotal role Birmingham has played for centuries in the global arms trade.

Not that you would have felt like celebrating if you were unlucky enough to hear that jet scream overhead, during its working life.

Past more little workshops and warehouses, the River Cole path plunges into another bucolic urban nature reserve. From time to time, the grey upper sections and gaunt chimney of the Tyseley Incinerator, burning the bulk of the city's waste, appear in the distance.

At the Acker's Trust the path parts ways with the River Cole, which continues its perambulation northwards to its confluence with the Tame, and eventually the Trent.

By now I am pretty much level with Digbeth but several miles to its east. Joining the towpath of the Grand Union Canal — the final waterway of the walk — I begin heading west.

I walk on through Tyseley, Bordesley Green, Small Heath, districts fully developed and integrated into Birmingham in the 19th Century. They form part of the city's kernel, its beating heart. Home to surviving rows of inner-city terraces, the ghosts of mighty firms like BSA, which produced first guns and then motorcycles, as well as St. Andrew's football ground.

It has always been an area where recent arrivals in the city set up home. After the Irish, it was people from Pakistan, India, and Bangladesh. More recently Somalis, Afghanis, Yemenis have joined the mix.

These neighbourhoods were heavily bombed during World War Two as the Luftwaffe targeted the area's cluster of large and small factories. After the end of the conflict the Council earmarked much of it for total redevelopment. Countless terraces and redbrick Victorian factories made way for maisonettes and part concrete, part metal industrial units.

Wholesale redevelopment brought sorely needed improvements to basic living and working conditions. But like antibiotics wiping out helpful gut bacteria whilst killing off an infection, redevelopment inflicted spatial dislocation on the inner city, destroying an organic fabric which had developed over generations.

Main line canals, like the Grand Union, were a different story. In the mid-20th Century, as freight transport by barge and narrowboat came to an end, the public authorities generally saw canals as insanitary ditches. All the better for filling in.

Consequently, the post-war redevelopment of inner Birmingham – prior to the 1980s, when the waterways were first rehabilitated as a pleasant amenity – largely swerved the city's canals. This has led to fascinating survivals all along the Grand Union Canal. Not least, canal wharfs here and there, complete with awnings, warehouses and turning circles, as if water carriage stopped yesterday as opposed to over 60 years ago.

Passing under a mighty blue metal railway bridge, I enter a wide section where bargees once marshalled their crafts for a final run on the central city wharfs. Perched on the brow of a small hill ringed by dual carriageways, stands the absurd structure of the former Church of the Holy Trinity in Camp Hill. Built from mellow limestone, this early example of a gothic revival building was constructed by the Church of England in the early 1820s, just as Birmingham began sprawling east into the

Warwickshire countryside. It looks like the kind of summer palace an Elizabethan or Jacobean aristocrat on the make would have erected at great expense, simply to allow their visiting monarch to play tennis or watch plays, before demolishing it upon their departure.

Following the towpath under Bordesley Middleway, there is an excellent brick mural of a canal boat, skilfully created by its sculptor in a faux naïf style, presumably as part of some distant regeneration project in the far-off 1980s or 1990s.

Beyond the Middleway, I enter the final stretch of the walk into Digbeth. Well preserved, the canal flanked on both sides by some still operational factories, I cross Bordesley Junction, where a canal arm lined with former workshops heads off to the north and the east.

Around here is the boundary between the eastern inner suburbs and Digbeth, which, like the Jewellery Quarter and the Gun Quarter to the west, can be properly considered part of central Birmingham. Every wall along the towpath is painted with graffiti – much of it pretty good.

The work of these street artists attests to the transitional moment in which Digbeth is currently caught up – the first new-build flats and warehouse conversions staking out its forthcoming property-led gentrification have gone up, yet still a lot of empty capacity and relatively cheap lets for art galleries, practice spaces and start-up breweries remain. Nearing the end of my walk, I pass the well-preserved former warehouse called The Bond, itself in the process of being extensively renovated – again.

The canal then fords the deep culvert carrying the River Rea – undoubtedly Birmingham's answer to the Thames, the Tiber or the Hudson – off to the north. The Rea's fast flowing waters were first harnessed here to mill crops and metal alike.

Birmingham was free from the strict craft organisations that existed in many older towns. The influence of the church and landed gentry – whose power centred upon Warwick, Coventry, Lichfield, Stafford, and Worcester – was felt lightly too. In fact, Birmingham was something of an outlaw town, a bit lawless, sprawling, everyone turning their hand to everything. It benefitted from nestling at the messy jurisdictional and cultural crux where Warwickshire, Staffordshire and Worcestershire bled one into another.

Just after the River Rea, on the left-hand side of the canal, lies Minerva Works. A former factory complex which is now home to numerous art galleries, event spaces and studios. Such as Centrala, VIVID Projects, Grand Union and Stryx. This makes these mid-20th Century former industrial units, sat at the junction between waterways, a key hub for art and culture in Digbeth. They keep alive the spirit of agglomerated, interconnected creativity which has animated Digbeth, Birmingham and the wider West Midlands, since the Middle Ages.

Between another former canal wharf frozen in its early 20th Century moment and the junction where the Grand Union connects with a branch that takes it up and around the edge of the city centre, a squat dark brick building comes into view.

This pretty nondescript structure is the Junction Works, constructed in the late 18th Century as canal company offices and it's been added to and altered ever since. In use for over 200 years, it is arguably Birmingham's oldest purpose-built office block and will continue to be used as office space for the foreseeable future. Courtesy of a £3.25 million funding package, Grand Union contemporary art gallery and studios are in the process of renovating it into new office space, studios, and an art gallery. It is expected to open in the summer of 2023, renewing Digbeth's ties to the canals and rivers which have shaped and given life to the district for decades.

Turning onto the stubby end of the Grand Union Canal branch, which ends at the crumbing former wharfs of the derelict Typhoo Tea Factory – itself due to be repurposed as offices and studios by the BBC – I pass a little community garden, nestling amongst grass at the side of the towpath.

As I approach, a young woman is walking towards me, coming down from Fazeley Street. She is dressed in the curatorial uniform du jour of a navy-blue French worker's style jacket and hard-wearing chinos. She carries a set of gardening tools and enters the garden. This plot is part of the Growing Project – another Grand Union art gallery initiative – focused on urban and community gardening and food growing. Another sign of growth and repurposing along the waterways of Birmingham, right in the heart of the city.

I head up onto Fazeley Street.

From here I can either walk down into Digbeth or pick my way through the High Speed Two works up towards the city centre.

Endless possibilities, created by the waterways and the city's ebb and flow.

Cup Song

BEN WADDINGTON

October, AD *641*
Woodland outside Beorm, Mercia

'Like this, Dudda.' Godric sharpens a stick with slow and careful downward movements of his knife. The younger boy, sitting astride an oaken log, tentatively repeats the movement with his own blade but the bark remains intact.

'Let me see,' Godric says, taking the knife from Dudda and testing the metal edge with his thumb. The blade is dull and the knife looks like it may have been buried for a time. 'Where did you find it? This spoon is not going to cut anything!' Dudda looks wounded. Godric feigns pitching the useless tool into the stream that babbles alongside them, but then gently returns it. The knife is surely a gift from a father who doesn't yet trust his son with a keen blade and Godric sees that the gesture is important. Using Godric's blade, Dudda slowly but diligently works the wood to a point. After some minutes, he proudly presents the stake to Godric, who approves with a smile. Dudda is then tasked with gathering further sticks while Godric whittles them at a brisk and practiced pace.

The two young hunters have followed the stream from their village since daybreak. The autumnal woodland quickly becomes unfamiliar away from the water and Godric must navigate by a nearly invisible network of deer tracks and by the careful placement of markers, jabbed into the ground at regular intervals. At the age of twelve, he has become comfortable making these navigations alone and their village leader Beorma acknowledges that even he doesn't roam so far. Today he is accompanied by Dudda, aged ten, who is yet to discover his makings in Beorm; a craft or aptitude that he can return to the village. Dudda is good with the making and placing of the sticks but the deer tracks are invisible to him until Godric patiently points them out, shows a tree's gnawed bark or pulls an antler from the grass.

Having rested, and with the sun now at its highest for the day, they again set out amongst the trees.

'How far will we follow the deer trail?' Dudda asks. His curiosity is real but the question is to break Godric's silence, a boy who in woodland naturally falls to stillness. In the woods, there is always something to hear.

'To the end of the valley. The woods will then become less dense.'

'Oh! How far is the valley?' The word clearly means something to Dudda.

'We're in the valley now!' Godric replies with a laugh.

Dudda looks left and right, in delight and confusion, not seeing the valley of his imagination.

'Look,' Godric gestures with his planed hands, brought together to indicate the gentle gradient of the land around them. 'What do you think a valley is?'

'I only know them from songs.'

'How do they look in songs?'

'They are steep and long and hard to walk through.'

'They can be but not round here. Go north for those valleys. And this walk is only easy for deer!'

Dudda pauses, then asks: 'Don't you know the songs?'

'Some. Not all boys sing.'

'You don't sing?'

'Only birds should sing in the woods.'

At this, Dudda maintains a moment's silence and clearly hears the fragile sounds that Godric hears. However, he soon resumes a muted version of the song that has accompanied them on their journey so far. Godric recognises it as a hunting victory song but in Dudda's version the woodland animals are keenly aware of the drunken hunters' rowdy arrival.

Today, the boys too are hunting but not for deer. In their village, everyone can find fruits and berries, even Dudda. They know where to go, when to look and what to avoid. From his grandmother Hlossa, Godric has gained a rarer knowledge. He has early memories of Hlossa waking him on Autumn mornings, then following her footsteps through the dewed grass into the woodlands beyond the wheat. She taught him a song unknown outside their family, a song more like a prayer, asking Erce to grant a good mushroom harvest. Their family enjoyed and respected this seasonal source of food. Familiar yet strange; plentiful and delicious. There were poisonous mushrooms too. 'So too are the berries that we gather and eat,' Hlossa would say to their uneasy neighbours, fear-frozen over a hot stew.

However, unlike the fruit they collect, and unlike the wheat they grow, the mushroom harvests are far less certain, with years of plenty followed by years of absence. Sometimes, deep into the woods, Hlossa believed someone had been there before them and was unsure if they had crossed a tribal border. 'Don't come back here, Godric,' she would advise sternly. Godric would remember the location and return the next year for a bountiful and unchallenged yield.

For those that know their names, the mushrooms describe the sublime, solemn or fleshly aspects of life: Morning Flame, Glass Ear, Boys and Girls, Earth Egg, White Veil, Liar, Black Antler, Prick, Night Tooth, Dead Boy. This morning, Godric is set on fruits he knows as Gold Cups. They are vivid in shade, their taste rich and piquant. They are uncommon and Hlossa knew only one remote place where they grew, but there they grew in abundance. Despite her promises over successive autumns, she never showed Godric the route. In woodland, in this season, precision is everything.

They thread soberly through the trees at a pace unsuited to the temperament of Beorma's other hunters. The woods are now golden with leaf-fall, making the cups more elusive. Over a mile, they find many but leave more: too young to cut or already eaten by the woodland's many tiny mouths. Godric feels that his eyes would be dulled by the collection of these lesser fruits, eyes that today feel as keen as his knife. The knife is there in his mind as they enter each glade and meadow, further sharpened with each find. Breathing in, Godric stops, kneels and gently uncovers the leaves ahead of him. His knife frees the hidden fruit where the stipe meets the moss. The cups they gather are placed gently in a felt sack, dyed a deep green by Hlossa. To Dudda, these golden revelations look like the magic of stories.

'What did you *see*?' he asks.

'Everything that calls the cups to grow is here. The trees, the soil, the grass, the leaves. The colours.'

'The wind,' offers Dudda, recalling a favourite song.

'No,' Godric smiles 'Not the wind.'

Such discoveries silence Dudda for minutes; he falls behind deferentially, then reappears in song alongside Godric, celebrating their quest, their yield and the knife that slices mushrooms from the earth. Godric has only heard songs of knives that cut men. Through the day, Dudda's verse celebrate the knife's utility in woodland and hearth settings, gaining the name 'Slix' and growing in fame through the land and down generations.

After some further miles of song, and the careful placement of the sticks, they reach an elevated, open meadow knotted with dark, mossy tufts. Free of the leaf blanket, the cups are visible in troops, always within an even distance of the trees. The boys work quickly around this ring from opposite directions. Dudda's quiet song on the still air allows Godric to follow his friend's progress while focussing his eyes on the ground ahead. Completing the circuit yields a generous harvest and gives a finality to the day's quest. Lying at rest, Godric feels a glow, anticipating Hlossa's joy at seeing their bounty.

'Give this place a name, Dudda. We will surely return.'

'Gold!' is Dudda's succinct suggestion, holding up the open sack.

'Gold Hill?' A smile from both boys fixes the name.

'And now we should return to Beorm, Dudda. Look how much of this day remains,' Godric gestures to the white sun, now lower in the sky. 'We have far to go.'

They follow the hill's crest to the meadow where Dudda jabbed their last – and now first – wooden path marker.

After walking some way across the level land and with Dudda singing of their shining triumph, Godric still doesn't see it. He slows his brisk pace, then stops. Dudda's song continues with a hesitant note. Godric turns to face the ridge, to align the path they took with his memory of it. Deep breaths quell the rising nip of doubt. He remembers something: the remaining sticks that he left neatly laid out are also missing. Dudda's song stops, leaving only the sound of the cawing rooks.

Neither boy wants to give voice to the mystery.

Godric walks towards the tree line, in search of the second marker. So quickly into the unknown. Dudda is the first to speak.

'It must be here somewhere, Godric,' his voice threaded with doubt.

'Are you asking me or telling me?' Dudda does not reply to the sharp tone. 'That we can see neither is our clue.'

'Can we still find the way?' asks Dudda to a silence. 'We could look for the holes,' Dudda suggests but only the rooks reply.

Godric wants to walk and think, and to get amongst the trees. But he feels keenly that he is walking without certainty. The unfamiliar woods now have the cold stab of danger. 'Let's find somewhere to sit and think. Do you still have some bread? I have two apples.'

Ahead, amongst the woodland's verticals, is a conspicuous horizontal: a fallen ash that has dislodged other boughs on its way down. One such thick branch invites them to rest. Dudda straddles it, facing Godric and humming quietly as he unwraps his last crust, his hopeful song still alive. He bites and chews, silencing the tune. Their thoughts are now accompanied only by the rooks' dark, dry sounds. Dudda swallows and voices the thought that occupies them both.

'Someone wants us lost.'

'We don't know that, Dudda.'

'Someone saw us gathering the cups at Gold Hill,' he says sadly; their first use of the name is as contested land.

'We don't know that we were seen there, or even that someone would care about Gold Cups. Let's talk instead about what we do know. Certainly without our markers we can't return the way we came. But we did not see who took them and we don't yet know why they did.'

Godric takes a bite of his apple and chews in thought, looking ahead through the trees to the ridge.

'We are half a mile from Gold Hill: we should not gather that we were seen there. I saw many wormy cups there, did you? Not what I would expect to see at someone's favourite hunting ground. We had our pick, even late in the day.'

Another bite of the apple's tart, pink flesh.

'Who might come this way and what might they think of our sticks?' Godric asks.

'They were our path!' Dudda cries. Godric passes him the other apple.

'Think as him, not as you.' When Dudda moves to speak, Godric gestures for silence and holds up his unfinished apple to say: 'Let me eat.'

When both apples are gone, Godric repositions himself on the branch to face Dudda.

'You are walking through the woods one day and you find a stick thrust into the ground. What would it tell you? What would you do about it?'

'I would know that someone was nearby.'

'You would not know how long it had been there.'

'I would see the next one nearby,' Dudda says.

'Yes, if your eyes were keen. However, you would not know it was a path.'

'I would follow the sticks.'

'If you had the time. You might be curious, but you would also be cautious. If you were bold, and considered this to be your ground, you might remove them.'

'Is this someone's wood?'

'All woods belong to someone.'

Dudda absorbs this and is silent for a moment. Then he asks: 'Am I a hunter?'

'No-one else would be out this far.'

'A hunter from Beorm?' Dudda asks, but their own hunters are not so intrepid. Both boys chuckle but the hunter's origin and current position remains unknown. Dudda puts one hand to the back of his neck, feeling where an arrow would enter it.

'Dudda, have hope. I know how we can return. We don't need our sticks or the deer trails and the sky is on our side.' Dudda looks up, quizzically. 'By night, the moon will light the woods and the stars will point the way. We will find the stream, which will then take us to Beorm. But we will have to walk far and walk true, like an arrow's flight.' Sensing Dudda's doubt, Godric adds: 'And we will need a song.'

Dudda's doubt turns quickly to shock as he spots something behind Godric. 'Look!' he cries, jumping from the bough.

Godric spins in alarm, expecting to see a man or an animal. Dudda darts over to the outlying branches of the fallen tree and reaches for something hanging there. The thin branch springs back gently into the air as he plucks it.

Dudda returns to Godric with unconcealed wonder, holding a small but exquisitely crafted bow. Godric breathes again and turns the bow over in his hands. Patterns have been scored into the wood all over its surface, but its most obvious feature is its size: this bow has clearly been made for a child.

'Godric, a *child* has taken our sticks. He thinks it's a game!' Dudda laughs, his whole body transformed by glee. Godric, however, is still cautious.

The bow is beautiful. Beorm too has bows this size, but they are roughly hewn and barely more than toys. Godric has not seen a bow so richly patterned. He thinks, 'Who made this?'

'Imagine this is yours,' he says, returning the bow to Dudda.

'I would come back to find it.' Dudda says.

Dudda gently draws back the taut bowstring with a finger, the bow comically small even in his young hands.

'Too young to be in the woods alone.' Godric voices his thoughts with a renewed urgency. 'You are here with your father. He wants you to become a master hunter, like him.'

Dudda examines the decoration on the bow, patterns that now tell the story of a small boy's destiny. His hand rises again to his neck and this time Godric too feels the keenness of that invisible arrow. Godric takes the bow from him and says: 'How did the bow hang; like this?' Godric reaches to a man's height and pulls down a twig to replace the bow. 'Good. Now, let's go.'

He puts his hand to Dudda's back and guides him gently away, deeper into the woods. How wrong that movement feels to him, but surely safer than awaiting the returning hunters. He senses Dudda is waiting for his words and their brisk gait easily loosens a story.

'You are walking with your young son, walking and hunting. All day you have been alert for movement but now you need to rest your eyes and your feet. Through the trees ahead, you see movement and gesture to your son to remain quiet. Two boys push a stick into the ground, then ascend the slope ahead. You remain seated, your stillness hiding you. Then you walk with your son over to the stick, and find more lying there, sharpened to points. You think: are these weapons? Are these boys or men?'

Dudda is silent but alert, deftly stepping through the springy undergrowth.

'Your eyes, now rested, spot another stick closer to the treeline. Keeping your son close, you follow the markers deeper into the woods. You are now focussed on the trail and forget that your son should also be carrying a bow.'

'Maybe you follow the boys, watch them gather mushrooms, then return to remove the sticks,' Dudda suggests.

Godric now is silent. Godric holds the cups close, wanting to keep his piquant purse; the day's only prize. Godric continues: 'You are familiar with the woods, enough to hunt here. This is your land. You see the sticks are not weapons, but a trail, and you know where they lead. Where else? They lead to Beorm.'

'What does it mean to you? Cups being taken from your land,' asks Dudda.

Godric stops to answer: 'Nothing or everything.' Godric has seen how quickly tribal instinct can blaze, has seen Beorma's own blunt fury at poachers and outsiders. They must return their harvest where it will be found.

Returning to the bow feels like walking upstream, against the current. It is Dudda who first sees the fallen tree and the bow hanging low like a fruit. Godric gestures for Dudda to stand back, while he slowly approaches the fallen tree. Imagining himself being watched, he holds out the sack, rolled back to reveal the nested, yellow contents. He places it carefully on the ground beneath the bow. Then treading back to Dudda, they again retreat into the woods, each step reducing the unseen threat. They leave Gold Hill behind forever, with less than when they arrived.

They walk without song or word until they feel certain they cannot be followed. As they await nightfall, Godric shows Dudda how to build a fire and – once dark – how to light it. Dudda is astonished that this is possible. Godric cuts two long, straight sticks which Dudda then shakily sharpens them to points: staffs to walk with in the dark but also a defence against the wood's other mouths. The fire warms Dudda's spirits and he resumes the tune of his song, first as a low hum, then with words. A still and silent Godric smiles at Dudda's revised account of the hunt.

'Do you sing songs like this in Beorm?'

'No, I just sing the real words there. But I always think of other words to sing.'

'Dudda, you could sing like this for the King and his court. Ascop.'

'No!'

'Yes, I think so. They need voices and stories like yours.'

With night, Godric recognises the star patterns as they turn through the sky, all animals or weapons. The moon – now in its third quarter – rises, and its fragile light softens the blackness of the night. Their advance through thick leaf-fall is slow but the path is certain. All around them are the snaps, creaks and taunts of the nocturnal woodland. A second fire when they reach an unknown brook staves off low spirits and the cold autumn air. The boys' words are low and soft as the moon lights their breath and the water. Dudda suggests they sleep here under the leaves like bears, but Godric persists with their starry path to the river, knowing that such an alluring sleep would have no others after.

Round Here

ALAN BEARD

Here comes Lester, swearing at no one. He lives largely on Twixes, lager and dope while his Universal Credit lasts and only lurches out to get supplies: bread, Rizla. Tonight, though, the noise, the fuss, has drawn him out.

Our street.

There's Rog, killed a pedestrian while drunk and spent four years in jail. Now he drinks most of the time but doesn't drive any more. In good weather he sits on a deckchair at the front, in that little yard we all have, drinking, cans lined up at his feet. Has a tag that means he can't go far. Never says a word, lays his red balding head back to look at the sky.

'Don't know where he gets the money,' says Mum.

There's Ben, all smiles, sensible, 'sunny', sane, no matter what, but his kids are wild, all over the place, in jail, doing drugs, God knows what. Apart from Charlene, the eldest, who is rich, married money and lives on some tropical island. She comes back every two years or so laden with gifts. As slim and brown as we remember. (We boys and girls have watched her walk by for years). Once the gift was a car. The whole street is always asking when's Charlene coming back? Do you remember last time she was here she wore a hat? Bought that ring for her mother? Her perfume.

After that it's the group of students, who change every year, sometimes every term. Tonight, they have the door open, bringing snacks and bottles and vape sticks out to sit on the low wall, or stand on it to get a better view.

Then there's the two most important houses, Sarah's – who I've loved since I saw her at nine years old coming out of her house one night, her pigtails catching street light – next door to the Ravensfords', Jimmie's, and Jimmie Ravensford is up in the window looking down at us all and calling my name, calling me for help.

Saw Jimmie first in the concrete park 5 years ago, we were both 10. He was dressed in a black hoodie and grey tracksuit bottoms, holding a plastic bottle half full of a yellow milk drink, pushing himself back and forth on the baby swing. A head popped over the 8 feet high wall behind him. Peaky Blinders haircut, Blues shirt. 'Hey you coming – they're fighting inside. Big fight.' The head became arms, body, legs as he climbed to the top of the wall, walked along. Nonchalant. He spat expertly. 16-ish. Jimmie, on the swing, looked up from his daydream: 'What? Hitting?'

'Yeh, come round the back or Dad'll get you.' Fat white trainers doubled the size of his feet.

Now he – Jimmie's older brother and protector, Dave – has gone.

I was jealous they had a dad until I met him. He would let me in when I called round. The dad, razored black hair, glasses, always looked on the verge of snapping. He greeted me not with words but a kind of humming. He crossed his arms a lot, gripping the elbows. I'd heard him really rip into Jimmie. So different from his mother, who was pale with dyed-white hair – blonde gone wrong? – piled up but wispy like a small cloud unravelling upwards. A ghost. Somehow, she'd uploaded a video of herself trying to work out Facebook and her strange antics – patting down her hair and stroking her face while shouting at her phone and playing with a removable section of her teeth – went viral, on everyone's phone at school. It was another reason to bully or shun Jimmie – now Dave wasn't around to protect him – on top of the smell of him, the same holey jumper worn every day for months, and the lack of anything to offer – food, fags, footie skills. They'd – we'd – mimic no-teeth talking, ummmmnn, ummmmnn over anything he had to say.

His spartan house had – has – a smell like stale biscuits and cat piss, though they had no cat (nor biscuits, come to think of it). The road's kids were scared of his dad but Jimmie said not to be, he wasn't all bad, there was a sled in the shed, he had things he liked and looked after, silvery ornaments in a cabinet in the front room where I wasn't allowed. I was always ushered out the back where Jimmie was trying to put a bicycle together, bits and pieces gathered, unscrewed, or found in bushes round about – a wheel here, a chain there – to add to the rusted but cleaned-up frame he'd got from somewhere. I helped him and although it was obviously never going to be roadworthy, we were both delighted when we got a wheel to rotate, or a brake pad to work. We jumped up and down like footballers celebrating goals, jabbing the air. Bad Dad would shout for us to shut up, loom up like a blot.

Jimmie told me his dad hallucinated enemies everywhere – he had pills for it – and his mum was going to divorce him: she couldn't take any more. I couldn't imagine the quiet woman, apart from the shouting-at-her-teeth viral video appearance, having the strength to do that, but she surprised me and got him kicked out of the house. The police came round to enforce it. She had to go to court. She withdrew more and more as the process was going on, head down when she opened the door to me, but I think she was glad I still came round, because Jimmie had fewer and fewer friends.

Go around the back of the shops, past the Mosque, and as long as I've been alive there's been a square mile of waste space, half demolished factories, piles of brick and abandoned hills of sand, intersected by roads, boarded up. Bridges carry trains beyond into the lights of Digbeth. Slowly the boards have rotted in the years-long rain and wind. Down a track at the back are the old garages where we all meet. They all meet. A few sprayed scrawls on the walls pass for decoration, old sofas dragged here to sit on. One night last year I went down there, some older lads/men in one unit, hip hop blasting, things passed around; at the entrance was a rambling, scruffy big man with grey twisted dreadlocks down his chest, who said to anyone passing he'd headbutt them if they came any closer. Beyond him, inside, I could see Sarah – the once pigtailed Sarah – in the corner, being snogged (and groped? I couldn't bear to look) by Blare. Blare of all people, a lanky twonk with admittedly good tatts, ironically called Brains by everyone. Didn't he slur, didn't he sweat?

I went past and on to the lone garage in bushes and there was Jimmie, kind of gaffer-taped to an old car seat on ribbed concrete as twilight filtered in through the gap where the door should be, swirls of mosquitos strayed from Upton's pond by his face. The assembled were trying to spook him, he's the littlest, the dumbest, the neediest, the youngest (I'm next), he was crying a bit. They poked sticks, not knives yet, at him, thrusting suddenly, theatrically. Some were filming on their phones. He saw me and struggled free, ran to me, and they let him come, bored already, and I had to turn and go back with him.

It's all thanks to Mum: when the Ravensfords moved here, she stood on the street talking to them and invited both boys in, to meet me, but Dave never bothered. Jimmie came, at first once a week or so, then more and more, startled at first by the kindness offered (tea, biscuits, Mum called him love, touched his shoulder), but settling in to play on the PlayStation. She encouraged me to call on him, especially when she worked late on her other shift, so it was her fault we hung out. Really, I wanted to stay with the gang, the boys a bit older, with their scorn of the good and the Gods, and their love for blood and darkness, who'd boast and smoke and spit well into the night.

On the way back from those noisy garages we stopped under a streetlight, seeing the traffic flow by at the top, a steady drone and the stream of yellow and red lights like schools of fish passing each other and Jimmie babbled on about did I believe in God and the Devil, was Hell real? He'd been got at by the blonde evangelical who runs the foodbank (classmates ridiculed him for going there with his mother, but we'd all been that way). He was handling me, my arm, my shoulder, a need in the grasp, his face close and round like a moon with a hole in it, and I wondered if he really was gay as the older lads seemed to think, shouting 'hey bum boy,' / 'batty man', and was he coming on to me? I remembered our shared five years, at first arms wrapped round each other, wrestling, tree climbing, then playing video games for hours day after day, side by side, with distaste now.

But a few days later Sarah stopped me and talked a long time about what happened that night at the garages, although nothing about what she was up to. She'd heard I'd saved her poor neighbour Jimmie and seemed to think I was OK now. Fit to talk to. I was close enough to watch her lips move. It wasn't all down to me, Brainy Blare was moving on too, to some other, discarding her. He'd ghosted her since that night. Another muscled idiot, I thought, for, besides a fondness for Love Island and Strictly,

Sarah was faultless. I'd checked from my window: watched her approach, flicking and sorting her hair with her hands in her just-above-the-knee blue dress and white trainers like a piece of the sky coming down the path.

Playing the hero got her into my house when Mum was on evening shift. One time on the mess and narrowness of my single bed I was able to undress her, my long-held crush, my hands on her smooth flesh. I just wanted to look at her, I wanted her to stay where she was forever. We drank mum's whisky, lying uncomfortably in a dent and heap of clothes; we pointed out stars we didn't know the name of through the window. Though she had a go: Great Bear? Warrior's Belt? Then laughed to show she didn't know. I don't know much, she was always saying to hear me contradict her. You know everything.

More nights followed, Mum now on permanent shifts. Sarah replaced Jimmie: her clear gaze instead of his squint. The PlayStation put away. I sounded drunk to myself as I walked trickily down the street after meetings with her. I tried to avoid the residents: Ben giving me his large smile, Rog bringing his sky-stare down to look as if he saw a difference in me as I went past and others in groups and twos, dogs and pushchairs, who were bound to be talking of me. I was the centre of everything now Sarah was my girlfriend, although she didn't like me saying that aloud and was careful not to hold hands in the street. I persisted. I swung round her house her front door her shed and her yard round the back and praised her mouth that I'd tasted and her eyes and hair for their colours and lustre, like a madman listing his visions. She laughed, and said, 'More, more,' little hands raised. I stored every one of her gestures and sayings in a Sarah space in my brain.

She lent me a book but I skimmed the contents, enough to talk about character and plot, preferring instead to think about where her own fingers had been on the pages, a little spill of coffee from her cup.

One night we walked the almost mile by backroads under slender railway arches to Digbeth, admiring the detailed graffiti, a girl with the world in her hand, assorted psychedelic faces, slashes of colour and lightening, and gawped at the various vaping hipsters attracted by the craft beer places, the live music. We lapped up the lights and the thump of the bass coming from nightclubs in converted warehouses. Ubers pulled up to let spill dressed up people, falling over each other; groups at tables and benches filling every available corner. When we had money, we planned to come back and be dancing in strobe light too. We practised on the way home.

Jimmie belonged to no one, his brother and father gone and his mother there but not there, and took to trailing us around. He needed us and we always let him down. We laughed him off, shook our heads as he came up. He said to us once when we did let him speak that he could see his problem now, he knew he was a nuisance, but he'd change his ways and not whine so much. For the gang, not admitted in, he'd still steal stuff (keeping that pale face down he was so hard to notice), from the outdoors, from the post office and the supermarket, from St Martins market and Selfridges where they took him like a hostage on the bus.

So, tonight, we aren't that close when his own dad comes back and kidnaps him. Holds him with his hand behind his back at the bedroom window. I haven't seen a knife, but Ben is saying he saw a serrated kitchen one flashing. Jimmie is used to this role and plays it well. I'm sure I can see him winking at me, up there in his window, but maybe not, maybe it's a frown. His dad alternately shouts at us gathering, the police talking back up to him, and muttering and shaking his head at the stupidity of their questions and suggestions and the stupidity of us all.

I remember him comparing his sons – strength and I.Q. – and praising the absent brother and ridiculing Jimmie and telling everyone who came round (just me) how there was nothing there and pointing at him and then at his own temple. Nothing there, nothing, and then other times he'd tell me to look out for him, his protégé, who'll look like him later and fulfil his glorious genetic legacy and promise. (He didn't put it like that).

Police are outside, blockading the house. Jimmie's wispy mother has a blanket round her to anchor her in amongst the officers of the law, ambulance men. She will appear again in today's Twitter feeds and WhatsApp chats.

'Poor Jimmie,' Mum says, but also, 'poor Ravensford, everything happens to him.' She makes sure I'm OK before she goes off to the group of parents by the corner. Nobody uses Ravensford's first name, no one knows it. Everything *has* happened to him. Unemployment, drink, mental problems, crime, now this divorce. The usual lot, I think, but remember he was mugged once, too, not here, outside some pub in town. They stole nothing – he had nothing – but the attack left him with a twisted leg and that twisted face. Maybe that was the deciding factor, to make him like this, to kidnap his own son and hold him for no ransom, for the pleasure of negotiating with the police and the street and to tell us all to look out for him when he's back out of prison. He'll be bigger and better then: he'll be a force to be reckoned with and he'll track us all down, one by one, and cut our ears and/or bollocks off, depending on our gender.

Sarah and me stand in the crowd, among the parents and people with dogs who stand around chatting like it was a celebration, or maybe a visit from Charlene, with her siblings out showing off their new phones and designer trainers that will hopefully last until the next time she calls. The houses with doors and windows open. Any excuse to get out and gossip. Rog even leaves the confines of his yard, despite his tag, and says real words instead of the low growling people are used to, his throat creaking with the effort of pushing up talk. Lester is swaying and nodding to himself at the back: here's fresh entertainment. Sarah is flushed with excitement, not at seeing me for the second time today, but about someone we know featuring, *trending* on social media. 'It's all over Twitter, Facebook, Insta, someone's live-streaming it.' Showing me her phone. We look to see who it might be but so many are filming, including the students showing each other the record numbers of likes and emojis: hearts, open-mouthed surprise, redface and tears.

Jimmie at last opens the window and shouts down to me, 'Ian! Help!' but his dad pushes him out of the way, and shouts from his little mouth that we are all to fuck off or he will push his son to the paved yard below. I think Jimmie would probably survive such a fall, he has a certain roundness on his side, but also if we can get closer, right up close we could break his fall, if the police would just move back and get their patrol car off the pavement. Jump, save, storm the palace. Crisis over. He should jump instead of shouting to me. I could shout back, still could, declaring matehood, make him feel better, but something stops me. He's so annoying and in-the-way, someone I must stick up for when I don't want to. I'm not his adored and muscled brother. Move on, ignore him.

I grip Sarah because she will be my wife — I will be a delivery driver and she will be a junior clerk for the City Council — and we will live with Mum for a bit, save up. Once we get a flat or something, rooms, we will live together and be mature and responsible, won't we, and we could then say hello to Jimmie if he's survived his dad and invite him for tea and maybe he would be Uncle Jimmie to our kids – we'd have one of each, and maybe one of neither – as long as he stopped being so needy and pulling you down with him. We could laugh over the old times, the times he got kidnapped and punched but right now I'm snuggling into my girlfriend, into our coupledom. We are going to be the new childhood sweethearts on the block. Or are we too old for that now? I check to see where Mum is, thinking that she might come over and plead Jimmie's case, but I don't think she heard his shout, or saw his look that held in it our unrideable bicycle and when we played Street fighter 5, sat side by side whooping and swearing, eating her biscuits.

It is not enough for me to shout back and tell him we're still friends, that he still counts, but I might still. Sarah will like it. Mum would like it. Even the gang lads, the lads of smoke and dagger and sarcasm will probably take notice. For a while anyway, but then Jimmie's hostageship, his weak-featured circular face half-heartedly shouting down, will become just another incident that happened. Things like that are always happening round here.

Birds

CHARLIE ROSE EVANS

Somebody is arguing with the bouncer, swaying under a cobweb of outdoor fairy lights, failing to convince him that she is sober enough to get in. The factory ghosts watch the spectacle unfold from above, swinging their legs from the old railway viaduct. Still, the smell of custard persists – clinging to their grey fabric, burrowed under fingernails.

The ghosts have behaved like socialites today. Earlier, they attended a wedding from a bird's-eye view, tangled around the ceiling beams of the old factory, sharing handkerchiefs to weep into as the bride circulated the room below. Death has made them sentimental, softening some of life's self-protective calluses. The floors their boots once trampled have been laminated and glossed. Repurposed into something expensive and modern. As if it no longer belongs to them. Sometimes, when the building is filled with sweaty bodies and glitter, neon lights and bass, they float above it all; remembering their own rituals, how their limbs once navigated crowded spaces. The warmth of another person's breath on their cheek.

On occasion, they indulge in following the office workers out from marketing and graphic design meetings to their craft pizza lunches. Pull up a pew. Reminisce about the sturdy feeling of breaking bread, factory floor gossip sprouting legs and leaping from one tongue to the next. The heavy-lidded exhaustion. Aching spines. Huddling together around The Old Crown fireplace.

Sometimes they catch sight of their lovers' clothes in the vintage pop-up shops. They double take at the faces spray painted onto terracotta brick – sure that the features could be that of their mother, or childhood friend.

The weariest ghost stubs her cigarette out. She tucks the remainder into her pinafore, saving it for later, then breaks away from her comrades. The woman who was arguing with the bouncer has run out of steam and is now slumped alone on a bench, violet faced, her bag and jacket strewn on the concrete. Phone dead. Hiccuping. The ghost is remembering the trick she found to get rid of hiccups – how her daughter once brought a spluttering child home for her to cure. They sat him at the kitchen table. Brought a teacup of water to his mouth, upside down. Her hands are busy as she lowers herself down beside the woman, smoothing the lap of her creased clothes. The dust clears from her throat. She must find a way to illuminate a safe passage home for her.

Josie (Slight Return)

PATRICK BOYDEN

2005, The Dubliner, Digbeth

Because it was lunchtime, and the April sun was shining, it was hard to reconcile what I was seeing with the dark, noisy, smoky place with sticky carpet and, often, stickier tables that I remembered from thirty years back.

'This used to be The Barrel Organ, didn't it?'

The barman shrugged as he poured my Guinness. 'Dunno,' he said.

'Sure was,' said Josie.

Two weeks earlier

I had arrived at the crematorium half an hour early. Outside the main gate were several dozen camera phone-wielding fans, and inside the expected scrum of photographers. A couple of them indifferently snapped some shots of me.

I watched the funeral procession glide towards the main entrance, surrounded by the paparazzi. I went in and found a seat near the back of the crammed room and shortly afterwards, Rob Cashman's coffin, the undertakers and the official mourners slow-marched to the front. Amongst them was a striking black woman, someone I hadn't seen for at least thirty years.

'Josie,' I whispered.

1975

'Yeah,' she said, 'short for Josephina, my mum's choice and she's the only one who calls me that.' She spoke in a slight Brummie accent with Jamaican overtones, and was constantly mobile, touching the arm or hand of whoever she was talking to. Being on the other side of the table, I was a little envious. By any standard, Josie was stunningly attractive. She was tall with a slim but shapely figure, emphasised by her skintight blue jeans. She wore a short, black leather jacket over a distractingly loose, white blouse. While Rob was prattling on about his music, she looked across the table at me. She held my gaze for a moment before turning back to Rob. A second or two later, I remembered to breathe.

Her band, on before us, had been bad, with Josie's notable exception, and Rob had collared her as she stepped off the stage.

Rob Cashman and I had been school friends and, like thousands of other teenagers in 1972, we formed a band. Rob was lead guitarist and vocalist and was pretty good at both, although, unfortunately, not at the same time. I was second guitar; our mates Paul and Nigel completed the line up on bass and drums.

Rob wrote the songs; we did a few covers, mostly for parties as Rob's compositions were a little esoteric. We were good and it didn't take long to get a following round the pubs and clubs of Birmingham. However, during our third gig at The Barrel Organ, Rob forgot the words to one of his own songs, the band ground to a halt, there were a few jeers, until Paul hit the intro to *Whole Lotta Love*. That moment was enough for us to agree we needed another vocalist.

'I've seen you here before,' Josie said. 'You're good when you do the rockier stuff.' She slapped her hand over her mouth. 'Ah, shit,

I didn't mean the rest is not good, it's just my taste, I suppose.'

By the end of the evening, she was our new vocalist.

Our first gig with Josie was two weeks later. She stood legs astride, one hand on the mike, the other halfway down the stand, pushing it back between her thighs or clutching it to her, leaning towards the audience, drawing them into her performance. Her shoulder-length curly hair flew round her face, but never obscured her smile. At the Barrel that first night, we knocked them dead. The next gig got us a manager. Jimmy Bennett promised us that he'd get work outside of Birmingham and, more crucially, a recording contract. It wasn't entirely his fault that it never happened.

The first hint of trouble was with Rob. He still took lead vocals on some of his compositions but Jimmy suggested that Josie's voice was more marketable, not a good word to use in Rob's presence. Increasingly, I was pushed back into simple strumming as Rob, responding to the snub, extended his own playing.

2005

There were a couple of eulogies from the more well-known faces, chosen, presumably, because of their fame, rather than any close friendship. There was genuine grief, however, from Rob's mother and his sister Jane, hugging each other as the curtains closed behind the coffin.

After the service, the family, close friends and VIPs filed out. I followed the procession to the wake at a smart country club. I chatted with Rob's mum for a few minutes but I was anxious to speak to Josie. When Jane came to sit with her mother, I made my excuses and went to the bar where Josie was talking to a young woman – her PA, I guessed.

'Water?' she said, nodding at my glass. 'What happened to the Guinness?'

She was dressed simply and stylishly and looked ten years younger than her true age.

'You haven't changed a bit!' I said.

'Ah, the sweet talk again. I've missed that. What are you up to these days?'

'Teacher, department head. Of English in Cheltenham.' I seemed to have lost the power of speech. 'Um. Drink? Rum and coke, isn't it?'

'Sorry, but no, I'm going. I just wanted to say hello and, well, goodbye. I've got a gig in Guildford tonight and there's a car waiting.'

'You've done well since Digbeth.'

'Since that kiss,' she laughed.

'Yeah, since then.' Since that kiss.

'Well, I have...'

'I came to see you once, about ten years back, at Ronnie Scott's.'

'Really? Why the hell didn't you come and find me afterwards?'

'I was with Cheryl and she was reluctant to come in the first place. She insisted on leaving before your encore.'

'Bitch,' she said.

'Josie, we need to be going.' The PA tugged at her sleeve.

Josie gave me a rueful look. 'Sorry, I do have to go.' She hugged me. 'Been far too long,' she said, and gave me a brief, soft kiss. 'Let's meet up.' She grabbed the PA's Blackberry, pressed a few buttons before nodding in satisfaction. 'One o'clock, Wednesday the fourteenth.'

'Where?' I said, as she began to walk away.

'Where else?' she said, grinning over her shoulder.

Two Weeks Later, The Dubliner

'Rum and coke,' Josie said to the barman, while studying me. 'You're looking pretty good, considering you're about eighty.'

'Thanks, and you look fabulous.'

We sat at a corner table. 'Not exactly busy, is it?' I said. There were no more than half a dozen other customers.

After a moment, she spoke.

'Tell me about Cheryl.' She sat close to me on the bench seat, her thigh pressed against mine. I tried not to read too much into this.

'We just grew apart. After the band split, she insisted I give up any idea of being a musician.' I sipped my pint. 'Fact is, I'd already made up my mind. I actually enjoy teaching, although asking fifteen-year-olds to write three hundred words on Sydney Carton's motivation for taking Charles Darnay's place at the guillotine can be a bit dispiriting.'

'Dickens, yeah?' she said with a smile. 'So how did it end?'

'It just got to a point where the only thing we had in common was indifference. What about you? You married your producer, didn't you?'

'Yeah, but I'm trying to forget that.'

We sat in silence for a minute or two, watching the barman have a small argument with a customer about his change.

She clutched my hand. 'Why didn't you call me?'

1975

The set had gone well, despite Rob going off on his own path a couple of times. He and Jimmy were having a serious discussion, so I went to fetch the Transit. Jimmy so far had got us one gig in Coventry where we outnumbered the audience and there was no sign of a recording contract.

Josie was outside leaning against the wall as I backed up the van.

'I came out for a crafty smoke. Want some?'

She passed me the joint; I took a drag and passed it back.

'Shotgun,' she said, then took a mouthful of smoke. She put her hand on my neck and pulled me to her mouth, gently exhaling the smoke. She held me there, soft lips turning the hit into a delicious kiss.

We broke apart, but before we could resume the pub door flew open and Rob crashed into the side of the van.

'And fucking stay out!'

Josie and I stared in astonishment. The barman saw us. 'You two, get your gear and piss off!'

Cheryl came out a split second after Josie and I had separated, gave us a look, and went to talk to Rob.

Paul gave us the news. 'Rob told Jimmy he was crap, Jimmy told him he was a dinosaur, Cheryl got involved, there was a lot of shouting, spilt drinks, Jimmy fucked off and the barman grabbed Rob.'

The gig was the last time I saw Rob, although we had a brief phone call, a sort of *postmortem*, the week after. Four years later, he released a record which did OK, and by the end of the millennium he was one of the UK's best-selling artistes, as well as one of its leading arseholes. Drunken fights with paparazzi, walk-outs from interviews and a serious cocaine habit – the news of his fatal heart attack was not much of a surprise.

2005. The Dubliner

'I didn't call because I was confused. I wanted to talk to you, but there didn't seem to be a chance. We only saw each other at rehearsals and gigs and Cheryl was always around.' I could feel the third pint sitting on my empty stomach. 'Shall we get a sandwich or something?' I said.

'Fuck off, stop dodging the question. I spent the best part of a month waiting for you to call.' She wasn't angry, but there was a sadness in her voice.

'You'd never hinted before that you felt that way, and I didn't want to cheat on Cheryl.' Josie didn't respond. 'Why didn't you say something?'

That it proved to be the wrong decision had stuck with me for years, ever since Cheryl, in a blazing row after Josie's gig at Ronnie Scott's, told me she'd slept with Rob both before and after we'd married.

'I was a coward.' I stared into my pint. 'I could have found you, but I was scared stiff that all it was was the post-gig adrenaline.'

'I didn't feel that way. I wanted you so bad. That moment, when we shared the spliff, I set that up, right down to the shotgun. I almost wanted Cheryl to catch us, but Rob fucked it up.' She dabbed at her eyes with her sleeve. 'Oh, Christ, I'm sorry. Seeing you at the funeral brought it all back.'

Later, we walked back to New Street station.

'Where's home these days?'

'Marlow,' she said, 'it's almost on the same road as Cheltenham, the A40, just a few miles further along. You could probably walk it, at least in a day or two.'

'Think I'll drive, if it's all the same.'

She smiled and gently stroked my cheek.

'So…' she said.

A Homeless Woman in Digbeth

ZAHIRA P. LATIF

I've always felt that Digbeth saw me through many tough times. My encounter later that day with a homeless woman was an instance of Digbeth steering me through life, yet again. I got off the bus outside the Tesla garage in Digbeth after a two-hour session with my chiropractor in Kings Heath. I'd been commuting through Digbeth much of my teenage and adult life. Most of the buses I caught during this time ran through Digbeth. As far back as I can remember, Digbeth was a gritty part of Birmingham city centre, marked by derelict buildings. It's now developing into a bohemian district, home to street art, cafes, independent shops, cinemas, and art venues.

My back problem had returned after four years. The last time, I was in a job I hated. For that job, I commuted at least four hours a day on the trains. This time I'd been in my current job for two years and I was quite frustrated. Thankfully there was no long commute for this one, but I wanted to move on. I liked my colleagues, but I was just no longer growing in the role. I believed my job was making me sick. Like last time, my back was the first place to show signs of stress. During this time, symptoms of irritable bowel syndrome (IBS) — an invisible, chronic, relapsing, and lifelong disorder of the lower gastrointestinal tract — reappeared. I was also constantly irritable and rather snappy with loved ones.

I was in excruciating pain before I went to see my chiro. Rose was good at fixing the pain and I left the clinic feeling like a new person. She gave me all the spiel about how I should minimise stress in my life, maintain a good posture and wear boring but comfortable shoes. Those of us with back problems receive this sort of advice all the time, and thanks to the daily grind of life, we never pay heed.

I dropped by the Zen shop. This is one of my favourite places in Digbeth, maybe even in Birmingham. Owned by Sylvia and her daughters, the Zen shop is a spiritual retailer selling crystals, incense, crystal jewellery, etc. I used to buy crystals often. I was going through a stage in my life where I was into New Ageism. There were parallels between my new interest and my own upbringing in a Muslim family following the Sufi tradition. New Ageism is an eclectic belief system, borrowing from many spiritual and religious practices. I loved crystals: big ones, small ones, smooth ones, wonky ones, even the rough ones.

I was beginning to develop into a bit of a crystal connoisseur. I would buy them as birthday and Christmas gifts for friends, family and even work colleagues. I bought a citrine crystal necklace for a co-worker, and she ended up having the pick of two job offers. I gave another two co-workers crystals, and both ended up excelling at work. Another colleague ended up pregnant with twins. I was convinced that this was no coincidence.

I spent some time in the shop, looking around for new crystals. I was after a gift for a friend but was unsure which crystal would be suitable. The retail assistant recommended a few. The conversation swiftly shifted to spirituality. I made a comment about how the New Age spiritual scene in Birmingham was predominantly situated in largely middle-class leafy suburbs and moaned about how it was inaccessible to me. She smiled and I smiled back, before paying for a few crystals, and wishing the assistant a good day.

As I walked past the Rainbow pub and was about to cross the Adderley Road, I saw a woman in a hijab on the other side, struggling with a large trolley suitcase. I asked if she was alright. 'Please help me, I have asthma,' she replied. She showed me a small piece of paper with an address in Handsworth on it and enquired which bus would take her there.

I advised her that she was best to take a taxi as she'd struggle with the trolley on the Birmingham buses during rush hour. I gave her the number of a local taxi firm and she pulled out her phone to call. She only had £9.00 on her and asked if it would be sufficient for her fare. I had no idea but suggested that she spoke to the taxi firm. She was on the phone for a few seconds before she hung up and said, 'They don't have any drivers available.' Thinking about my own experience, I realised that local taxi firms, at least those that were affordable, were generally unreliable and I ended up having to rely on Uber.

She was guarded and reserved; behaviour I had seen before. I had previously researched South Asian women's experiences of domestic violence – in fact, I had written a PhD thesis on the subject. Her behaviour resonated with that of my research participants. Short responses to my questions about what she was doing in Digbeth hauling a trolley suitcase got me thinking about my research participants' narratives. Many were forced to leave their homes as the abuse had escalated to a tipping point. When I met my research participants, they were living out of a suitcase in women's shelters, seeking permanent housing.

She had been thrown out of the family home by her parents. She told me that her parents didn't like her husband. I assumed she had entered the marriage against their wishes, but that wasn't the case. It was an arranged marriage. Her parents had introduced her to her husband. So why were her parents throwing her out? Because 'he won't dance to their tune', she replied. They had given her an ultimatum – *if you want us, you can stay, if you want him, get out.*

She was from Nottingham and ended up on the doorstep of a homeless charity in Digbeth. That's all I got from her, apart from 'you know Asian families' and 'I have a baby who is with my husband in Pakistan.' I suggested she call the homeless charity to get some help with booking a taxi. She did just that and was informed that a taxi would be with her in ten minutes. I waited with her.

Those ten minutes were the longest of my life – she said nothing. No attempt to make any conversation. Not even to cover the awkward silence. Small talk was probably the last thing on her mind. I had a million questions starting with why would South Asian parents throw their daughter out? As a South Asian woman myself, I understood that South Asian women represented their family honour. Why would parents disregard their honour? Just like me she was a Muslim woman. Islamic teachings on the treatment of women and specifically daughters were clear. Women should be respected, and daughters ought to be cherished.

Before I could get my head around it all, the homeless charity called her, informing her that the taxi was waiting for her in the car park of the Enterprise car rental firm. She shook my hand, thanked me for helping her, and made her way to the destination. I never saw her after that. I wanted to help but didn't know how. To come to terms with my feelings of helplessness, I made *du'a'*[1] for her, hoping that she would be reunited with her baby and husband. A part of me wanted to keep in contact with her

1 In Islam a prayer to ask for assistance from God.

and kicked myself for not exchanging contact details. But then there was the other side of me which felt aspects of her experience were a bit too close to home.

Somewhere in this homeless woman's experiences I recognised my own insecurities. Perhaps she was me in another life. I suppose many of us are one pay cheque, a few months of savings (for the luckier ones) and familial relationship breakdown away from being homeless. The homeless woman represented the fragility of modern life. In an instant it can all come tumbling down around us. That was what I was afraid of, and I had momentarily come face to face with this fear. My encounter with the homeless woman was no coincidence. It was life screaming at me to beware.

I'm a divorced single woman living at home with my parents in their three-bed semi with my brother, sister-in-law and their two young boys. It's heaving in the house. My parents occupy the main bedroom; my brother, sister-in-law and the two little boys are in the second bedroom, while I am in the box room. My brother, a private and grammar school-educated graduate, hadn't held a steady job down for around two decades. A family milieu ripe for disputes.

I wondered how many families live in homes that are contested? Where emotions are high and tensions are rife? During my PhD studies, I had explored conceptualisations of home and homelessness. At the time I was hooked by propositions of home that encapsulated meanings beyond the physical structure of a house or the capital value it may represent. While studies support the authenticity of home as a social, psychological, cultural, and emotional phenomenon, this has been largely unrecognised in housing and homelessness policies in the UK. It got me thinking about how we conceptualise homelessness – mostly through public and social policies which prioritise a physical structure.

It was the work of an academic – Mike Seal – that resonated with me. Seal asserts that the more secure we are in our homes, the more we have security in our sense of self. Our social, political, economic, and cultural landscape works against ensuring we are secure in our homes. As Zygmunt Bauman argued, we live in liquid times, a state of endemic uncertainty with liquid love, emphasising the frailty of human bonds, and a liquid life, a precarious life which is lived in a state of endless uncertainty.

It was no coincidence that I bumped into that homeless woman; after all, Digbeth was home to a few homelessness charities. Digbeth has a history of welcoming immigrants. Historically, it was the Irish community who found salvation in the area during the potato famine. Until 1996, the St Patrick's Parade was held in Digbeth. Birmingham Coach Station, located in Digbeth, welcomed the homeless woman to Birmingham. Digbeth is the doorway to Birmingham for those deprived and disadvantaged by increasing inequality. How many more will escape the harsh consequences of the cost-of-living crisis? Digbeth cannot support them all.

My encounter with the homeless woman fired up my own desires. At the time, my one and only wish was to own my own home. Initially my drive for home ownership felt like it arose from the normalisation of home ownership in the UK, which I had put down to the neoliberal ideology of personal responsibility and consumerism. It was security that I sought and which I believed owning a place of my own would bring. Some years later I recognised that bricks and mortar were only partially going to make me feel secure. I drew parallels between my yearning to own a new home and my internal lack of security stemming from a world that increasingly felt unstable, insecure, and disconnected. Yet, ironically, we have never been so globally connected.

After bidding the homeless woman farewell, I waited for the number seventeen to pull up. Within a few minutes, I had left Digbeth behind only to find the bus gridlocked in traffic. It was a late Friday afternoon and people were in a rush to get home. My thoughts were with the homeless woman who was going to end up in temporary accommodation for a while before she would be able to secure a home.

About twenty minutes later, I arrived home and was greeted by Mum. I told her about the homeless woman. She listened before rhetorically asking, 'Why did the parents throw their daughter out?' Mum was also bewildered. Of course, the actions of the woman's parents went against South Asian Muslim family values. At one point Mum even swore at the parents, before she rationally came out with 'families are in trouble' and Dad quickly interjected with 'brown families are in trouble.' I left the conversation before it got too close for comfort and took my cue to get on with some writing.

Eight months after meeting the homeless woman, I was at a job interview with a large charitable institute located in the back streets of Digbeth. This was my second interview at the organisation. I wanted a job with this charity, though at first I could not rationalise why. I would be paid less than in the private or public sector and possibly never be able to afford to buy a place. So why did I want it? I was torn between doing meaningful work, which I thought I could find working for a charity, and a job that paid well but was, as David Graeber puts it, bullshit. The charity, a humanitarian aid organisation, was supporting the homeless around the world.

The Parking Space

HELEN CROSS

It was just a paved over front garden in Digbeth, which offered space for two, maybe three, cars. No weeds between the speckled grey blocks, no moss or leaves, no natural border of soil before the brick wall. Just one solid, expensively sealed patch of the inner city.

'I couldn't possibly accept. For one thing, Justine, it's obviously a gateway drug to luxury living and I'm broke,' Hazel says.

'You won't be going *inside* Nadia's house,' Justine replies. 'You'll just be *parking* here. You'll be arriving by 8am and gone by 6pm. Boom. I don't understand what the problem is.'

'Look at me. I'm in danger of losing a leg to diabetes. The last thing I need is less walking, Justine.'

'Don't try that big girls' jolly shit with me,' Justine snaps, arms folded tightly against her chest.

'Look, I put on a lot of weight in lockdown, all right.'

'I was fat too once,' Justine says, touching Hazel on the shoulder. 'Many of us at The Closeness were. Now we work out. At the gym. Membership of which is included with your employment package. You know that, right? And it's fully re-opened. So there's no need for you to do all this walking.'

Hazel nods. She's seen on Fazeley Street a state-of-the-art boxing studio, and a repurposed warehouse, where she can learn aerial trapeze and other circus skills, safely in her lunch hour, for free.

'And there's no need for that self-deprecating boo-ha either,' Justine adds. 'You're in Birmingham now, girl. We're strong straightforward people. We've no time for bullshit and pretending.'

'Okay, well, in the name of no bullshit, no thanks. I don't want to park there. I want to walk.'

The next morning Hazel leaves her flat early and draws up before seven at Palmerstone Road. It is two long miles along a deserted towpath from the 'sustainable hub' which is her office. Hazel pulls on her anorak, waterproof trousers and rubber boots, and heads towards the Grand Union Canal. A rat, poisoned to a bloated lilo, bobs upside down on the scummy Guinness-dark water, teeny dead paws pressed together in a final namaste. Such sights had provided the inspiration for Hazel's only original storyboard so far this year ('*Run Rat Run; an epic battle of commuters and rodents*').

Hazel walks steadily, Vaselining her lips, brimming with fear, the end-of-day cans in her backpack clunking against her laptop. She eyes the rancid water and thinks of the mad friends who had taken up wild swimming and then wishes it were time to sit and fizz her cans open on a slimy bench. In the high distance silver cranes are beginning their slow swings again, and Hazel tries, without success, to work, to animate an avatar in that cab, a kick-ass sniper in the clouds, in a visor and a yellow helmet.

An hour later, and from some distance, several hard-bodied young workers from The Closeness gather to watch Hazel, followed by two Canadian geese, waddling, wet and wheezing, beneath a threatening sky towards their 'buzzing creative community'. They wave. A sharp-nosed train slides past behind them.

It has rained en route, and Hazel's not worn a hat (she has a hairdryer in her desk drawer), but before she can even slip into the disabled toilet to change, a text pings in: '*Let's just take a proper peep'* and Justine is at her side, slyly eyeing Hazel's muddy boots, then steering her across the road, back towards the parking space.

'Look at it. All of it.' They stand before the high Victorian Digbeth terrace, Justine's arms akimbo. The door is painted a steely grey, the brick walls thickly creamed, softly rounded as if dipped in white chocolate and frozen. Expensive corporate domestic. No letterbox. She thinks she'd not noticed that blatant security hazard go; gone the way of the handwritten letter, the lickable stamp, the milk bottle, the milkman, the handshake, the cheek kiss, lipstick, the budget airline, her mother, her marriage, her work-in-progress, her creative freelance career.

'The house comes with Nadia's job. It might be owned by Channel 4, I'm not sure. Maybe by the BBC. Someone said Sky. Netflix? I dunno. Or was it Sony? Microsoft? PlayStation maybe. But it's where Nadia, our Artistic Director, lives when she's in the UK, so in a way it belongs to all of us who work at The Closeness. That's why Nadia suggested you use it while she's away in America.'

'Why me?' Hazel asks and Justine purses her lips, shooting her eyebrows to her hairline.

Hazel knows that several youngsters glide happily into The Closeness on in-line skates. Another hover-boards, and she's seen a unicycle in the locker room. Most of The Closeness team are fit young city-walkers, with a splattering of coding oddballs who cycle, but a few still drive cars. So why the hell don't they park here?

'Nadia said you.'

'Just being in the parking space will... unsettle me,' Hazel says. 'I live in a one-bedroom flat above a butcher's in Hollywood.' In her living room is every piece of furniture the landlord owned in the Nineties, and in the fridge nothing but six cans of Waitrose elderflower cider. 'I can't start getting ideas even about the area where I want to live in this city. I can't start fantasizing about living in Digbeth.'

'Who lives in Hollywood? That's not the city.'

'Excuse me, it's officially part of this city.'

'It's a geriatric suburb.' And Justine gives Hazel the sort of smirk more normally associated with innuendo, as though she suspects Hazel is not just still isolating but holed up in Hollywood with a sex robot.

'John Taylor was born there. Duran Duran? A pop band from the Eighties? '

'What are you doing out there, Hazel? Practicing for a pub quiz?'

I'm trying to hold onto a fragment of myself as a solitary visual artist, she thinks.

'You only moved there so you can keep saying, "*I live above a butcher's in Hollywood*".' Justine mimics Hazel's voice rather accurately and the effect sounds meaner than she maybe intended, so Justine gives Hazel a quick anxiety-inducing hug. 'We just want to help you settle into us. Into The Closeness.'

Hazel agrees to reconsider, but at end of the day when she has refashioned into her waterproofs and is about to head back to the towpath Justine appears again. She is smiling this time, perhaps still feeling bad about her mimicking earlier. 'Just think about it,' she coos. 'It'll soon be the end of the summer days and you'll be wanting to go out with new people. In the city! We're all free now. You'll be having a drink with the team after work. Going to see movies at the Mockingbird. Hanging out at the Street Food Festival. You don't want two lonely dangerous miles of walking at the end of every day. Diesel fumes give you Alzheimer's, Hazel.'

'I need to lose weight.'

'You need to make friends. You need to loosen up. You need to settle in to Digbeth and The Closeness.' Then she looks at Hazel steadily and says, 'I think it's time.'

'For what?'

Somewhere sparrows, starlings and thrushes are suddenly heard laughing.

'You need to meet Nadia.'

Hazel looks around in panic but there is no sign of Nadia, who is rarely spotted but intimately known, particularly for her seamless success that has continued undented by *events*. Like an A-grade Aeriel she's girdled the globe with qualifications, gliding from the city's best grammar school, through BA English Oxford University, MA Virtual Reality, London College of Communications, PhD Film and Visual Studies, Harvard Graduate Tech Institute, Google, Apple, Pixel studios then, during lockdown back to her hometown, clutching a Channel 4 and Intel-backed *Covid Kick Start* business grant. This paid for the transformation of a filthy Digbeth warehouse into a state-of-the-art tech studio and urban jungle tranquility complex. From here Nadia fronts this city's bid for new digital 2025 unicorns via her own start-up: The Closeness. A company 'nourished by' digital narrative, high concept 3D games, 'gender enquiry and hologram performance art' (no rats).

All this according to The Independent's '30 Digital Innovators Under 40'. Though Nadia didn't look under forty. That cloud of black hair was forked with delicate lightning bolts, and she didn't make self-deprecating jokes, so she'd seemed at the Zoom interview (the only occasion Hazel has seen her), like an older witch.

'She's still in America,' Justine says, clapping her hands together, breaking the dream. 'Hol-O-thello,'s been a great success. The New York Times called it, '*Floating art for a reflective age.*' She's got the money for the Hol-O-Hamlet and there are plans for Hol–O-Henries 1-4. They're linking up with the Royal Shakespeare Company, Channel 4, Puffweasel Studios. There's going to be an app.'

What Justine doesn't understand is that Hazel needs to be away from corporate culture to be creative, and that night Hazel types Justine an email: '*Thank you for the kind, and repeated, offer of Nadia's parking space. However, this is an email to officially decline. If I can help in any other way do let me know. How about I live in the staff kitchen? Monday to Friday sleepovers in the green studio? No probs catching super rats with my big bare hands and toasting them with chipotle chilli in a fire-pit. You want to know the truth, lady? I walk to stimulate ideas. To re-adapt. To conjure my old mind back. And I drive so I won't be tempted to drink during the day. But drinking at night — and miscarriage, divorce, failure, the death of my beloved mother, alone in an infected care home, has made me overweight so I need to drive and walk and so this — this job this city this life — is my mistaken solution. I wish as much as you do that I didn't work at The Closeness. I wish I didn't live in this nowhere city which I left as soon as I could, at 18. I wish my old life in London hadn't been stripped from me and I'm sorry you made the mistake in hiring me and now I soil your so-called creative community; if my life hadn't fallen apart in London I wouldn't be here. I would be living in nappy-valley with my Olympic bronze-medal-winning husband. Maybe even having that miracle later-life baby by now.*'

Did Hazel then think better of it? Did she do the digital equivalent of screwing it up with a manic giggle and tossing it in a high arch into the trash? No. She'd had a bottle of Merlot and two M&S tins of G&T so Hazel pressed send, and off the email went to Justine.

The next morning Nadia is waiting in the parking space. Nadia! She has a tiny steel suitcase at her feet, and Hazel thinks it is for her, all the contents of her desk drawer tipped in, before she remembers that Nadia, her boss, despite just having returned from LA, is due that day to go, as part of the UK's *Fight! Re-ignite*! taskforce, to the reopened Bronx with the Hol-O-Thello. Still Hazel assumes Nadia is up early to sack her first. The humiliation couldn't even be presented as cost-cutting because The Closeness has just been given a sizeable grant as part of the *Big Bounce Back*, which is spearheaded by the UK's digital industries.

Luckily Hazel didn't care about being sacked. It would be a relief to get back to idle hours and the core business of being a true comic book artist: drinking herself to death alone in Hollywood.

'We just want to make things as easy as possible,' Nadia says in conclusion in some point that Hazel has missed. 'It is terrible what happened but life is flux. Everything changes. Catch that and fly, Hazel. At The Closeness we're a new sort of family and as you settle in, you'll trust us. We need you. Park at my house. Greet the breeze. Read Seneca on the good life. Get to know the new Digbeth, feel the city. If you are all at sea, drift beneath the stars as you must, but trust in the coming shore.' Then she spreads a jewelled finger behind her, in the parking space's direction, and, like she is directing traffic, extends her arm to its fullest length.

The game is up.

What Nadia suggests, people do. So, the next morning Hazel drives all the way from Hollywood to The Closeness for the first time since she started there, and parks in the paved space in front of Nadia's house. It is shallower than she'd expected and her battered VW Up! is nosed right up to the ivory windowsill.

On her third day of parking at Nadia's, a Friday, Hazel returns to the parking space to see that a blue wheelie bin is blocking her usual rear manoeuvre. The lid is tilted open over a mound of wine bottles. She tries to move it and, panting, notices the air is warm and smoky. Burning. Meat. Her first jumble of thoughts are versions on 'melting flesh' but there is no one around and then she sees a banner hung across the road, which announces *We're back! Over 50 Independent Vendors*. Half an hour later her jaw is wide and the grease is just spreading over her chins when she notices Alishba, a young co-worker, standing with another woman. They drift over. With cuisine from around the world on offer, Hazel has ordered the timid choice, a pulled pork burger with homemade coleslaw and a pint of artisan cider, but it's proving just as challenging as chopsticking through a plate of dumplings.

'How's it going?' Alishba says sweetly. 'Hey, Hazel's our Games Master. Before she came to us she did Puffin Patrol.' They both gasp and began to reminisce over Puffin Patrol.

'You live round here?' the friend asks.

'I live above a butcher's shop in Hollywood,' she says and the women laugh. Justine's wrong; it's good to have a joke prepared when you are Hazel's age with a tragic back-story and alone in a city you never wanted to return to.

'Can I get you another drink?' the friend asks but because of the driving, Hazel declines, though she is pleased by the offer. Her lost friends have all, one by one, given up drinking; after a mini stroke, a conviction for drink driving, a vomit scandal at a fiftieth birthday party and then pub-dread in Covid. Only Hazel kept going because it's part of being an artist.

'We live in the Jewellery Quarter,' Alishba says.

'Well, more of the Jewellery Sixteenth.'

'It's a very small apartment. You should come round one night. If we move the dining table out, we can fit three people in.'

'What are you running from?' the friend says and Hazel blinks, wondering if tears are spilling from the brim of her soft old eyes and she pats her pockets looking for a napkin and a sanitizer.

What is she running from? Death in general? Failure? Life as an older female artist? That which can never be outpaced? And she doesn't mean the physicality of early middle age; she's been round the track on that one and can't find deep pain in the wasting of her body or face. Then she realises the friend is smiling kindly because she had not said '*What are you running from?'* she'd said, *'What are you working on?'*

'A new game world. A midnight forest. From a dog's perspective,' she says, because she'd just remembered.

Next morning, Hazel parks and then sees a woman drift across the window of Nadia's house. The blinds are, for the first time, up. The figure, tall and willowy, tips her head forward, spraying over a long arc of black hair, which she down-brushes for a long time, until she flings the jet strands back over, silkier now. Then she stretches and disappears, perhaps in downward dog, from sight.

The next morning, Hazel is on the busy main street, indicating to turn into the parking space, when the door opens and the same woman, hair now tied up in messy bun, and wearing the golden hoops, high leather boots and the bright mini-skirt of the fashionable middle-ager, is leaving the house. The woman bobs down as Hazel unwinds the window. 'I'm sorry I've left a bit of a mess,' the woman says. Hair silvered at the temples.

A gash of red over dry lips. 'I didn't realise you'd be coming today.'

Hazel had been the cleverest girl in her comprehensive but when she met this type at university they'd hit her like a boot to the chest, and now she almost apologises, and says, yes of course, she'll happily return the next day for the cleaning. Then she recovers just in time to explain that she's not, in fact, despite appearances, the cleaner, just an employee of The Closeness using the parking space, and soon the two women speak quickly in the keen-to-be-liked clichés of female strangers meeting for the first time, the usual non-aggression pact.

Hazel establishes that the woman is Rebecca, a friend of Nadia's from the Oxford days. As Nadia is off in the Bronx, she's offered Rebecca the house, because Rebecca's London theatre furlough led to her being out on her ear when the company went bust, and two years on she's still adrift. 'And I'm not sure what I'm going to do,' she says quietly. 'I'm 47.'

'Same as me.'

'Then you'll understand.'

For a long moment the two women stare at one another as if mesmerised by a slow shift behind the screen of their faces: honesty maybe.

High above, the *whoo* of the wren sounds and Hazel remembers seeing satin in the rag market, foreign coins in the casino.

'Long ago when I was first making my films, I used to earn money at The Independent newspaper,' Rebecca says with a sigh. She leans back against Hazel's Up!, lights a cigarette, then as she smokes she addresses both Hazel and beyond her, the air. 'Film Critic. When the paper went down I went freelance with that too. Of course, everyone's a film critic now. It's hard to get any properly paid work. So, I had to get another gig as a dramaturg, unpaid for a long time, but eventually freelance but now that's gone because the theatre went bust so Nadia found me online and suggested I come here, back to Birmingham, though the library where I studied for my A Levels is under a corporate tower block. You?'

'A couple of graphic novels,' Hazel says, speaking a few words to the windscreen, before letting her head hit the steering wheel. 'I didn't make any money, or maybe I was just unpopular, or crap. I was dropped. By everyone. After I failed at that, and on the advice of rich male friends, I taught myself coding. I adapted, did animation. Had a few early hits with toddlers.'

'Then Nadia heard about you and brought you back to Digbeth? To The Closeness?' Rebecca says, turning to face Hazel, who lifts her head up and wipes her eyes. The women stare at one another bewildered, fumbling for an understanding, which is there but hidden.

'I just saw an advert in my inbox. I applied.'

'But how did she know you needed to be here?'

'I don't know.'

Then they rally through a few laughs about the difference in house prices (*'I'm putting in an offer on the whole of the Rotunda'*) and go their separate ways.

Hazel knows that if she were a character in one of her own games, she'd have just one round of bullets left.

'Nadia's back on Wednesday,' Justine chirps the next morning. 'It's all go Hol-o. Execs want to add a complementary suite of blockbusting Hol-o games set in period Shakespearean 3D England to release on St George's Day 2025 in a co-production with the yanks. Nadia's setting up an LA studio. Some of us will go out there. It could be you. Until then, demons. Cursed shields.

Floating swords. Bulging breeches. Witches. Ghosts. Portals. The rock hard, sci-fi side of Shakespeare, please. Of course, Nadia will use the profit from these games to pay for independent creative projects. The financial future of The Closeness and the resurgence of British culture are in your hands, Hazel. Nadia thinks you're ready.'

'Leave it with me.'

Hazel thinks she might kill herself.

Just a floating thought as she walks back to the parking space at the end of the week. She's tired and she's an artist and tiny madnesses take on garish forms, as they are hammered to blades against the anvil of the imagination, then baked to an ebony crisp by self-doubt. Such a mood is heightened because it's late and Hazel's been drifting around Digbeth for hours, comforted in some bleak way by the dirty tunnels, the blackened bricks, the perfect archways of abandoned viaducts. These gloomy relics, these damp shadows once were proud, had strength and beauty and busyness, and how Hazel wishes she saw some soaring metaphor for her own self here.

She notices the door to Nadia's house is inched open. The blue lights beating beyond the window turn the house to the sea at dusk. Her undergraduate degree had been in Earth Sciences and for three youthful summers twenty-five years ago Hazel had worked as a Visitor Experience Assistant with the Royal Society for the Protection of Birds at Bempton on the East Coast. One of her jobs was to sit in a boat out at sea and count the nesting seabirds clustered on the white cliffs. Kittiwakes, razorbills and puffins, a few fulmars, once an albatross. She made slim short marks for each sighting with a pencil. She'd been bored at first: but the rhythm of the waves, the counting, it had released her young self towards self-creation. She began to watch, then sketch, the birds, and these first pencil drawings led, years later to Puffin Patrol. She'd been happy then and, yes, *centred*, in her life, and confident of her future, and that of the planet. Despite being utterly alone and in danger for hours on end.

Now Hazel wants to help but more than this she wants a quick nosey peek inside the house. So she walks to the door and knocks. When there is no reply she presses the tip of her finger against the wood, her heart a balloon, as the door eases wider, welcoming her inside.

If Nadia, or the woman who has been in the house, Rebecca, has died what will she do? How will she excuse being still in the parking space at 11.08pm? How to explain wandering through the moonlit house of strangers at all?

Then again, if Rebecca or Nadia haven't died, if they have just collapsed with exhaustion from trying to get their lives started again, or gone overboard on consoling booze (there is definitely an air of booziness in this house) Hazel has overreacted big time by shouting out, 'Who's there? Come out!' at the top of her voice.

She walks deeper in. Until she sees a slink of movement and Rebecca creeping down the corridor muttering, shaking her head, one hand over sunken sockets, the other fumbling for the sunglasses in her hair. Hazel is surprised to realise she wants to hold the woman but, as she learns later, artistic failure, shame and adolescent stomach pumping has made Rebecca wired and prickly. So, Hazel just holds the stranger's cold hand, damp and smooth as an oyster, instead. She strokes the wrecked hair out of Rebecca's red eyes and they go to sit on the modular sofa in the silvered, moonlit living room.

It boils down to trying to be an artist in a world that doesn't care, to loneliness, anxiety, years of overdosing on solitude and the drinkability of Aldi's red wine, they agree. After Rebecca lost her furloughed job she had no money, which at first had worked in sobriety's favour, but now the chi-chi bars of Digbeth, where despair is easily presented as style, plus the artist's lingering preference for isolation, Nadia's superior inner-city terrace, the cash from the London house sale in her deposit account: it has all thrown Rebecca off balance.

'It's nothing I've not done myself. My best friend has been a bottle of Merlot for over two years,' Hazel says and they laugh for the first time.

It is soon 5am, and they could have parted, apologised and got back into their respective beds but they decide, because they are broken but together, to walk out of Digbeth towards the city centre for coffee.

'Nadia thinks,' Rebecca says, as they pass two teenage girls, cheeks pressed together carelessly, singing into one phone. 'That the future's almost here. And it's female.'

Blackbirds are starting up.

A lemon dawn is rinsing the grey morning.

It is getting light.

Pavement Chalk

JOEL BLACKLEDGE

Put a picture in your mind: a row of houses, like a single line of pale red brick patterned with doors and windows identical but for their dilapidation. Opposite them another row, separated by rough-worn cobbles but joined by washing lines, like rowboats tethered to a jetty. Behind each home was another, facing a yard built entirely of brick. It housed privies and a washroom: a view less attractive than the street. A Morris Minor passed somewhere out of sight, its raspy rumble weaving between the shutters and chimney stacks of Digbeth. This street, however, had no cars.

Mary sat on the front step of her house. She was drawing on the uneven pavement using a stick of pale blue chalk. It was the last surviving stick from the pack she had taken home from school in the summer. The day was cold and bright.

She was not yet accustomed to the quiet. The other families, who had always made the street a place of movement and din, had left. Their houses were being cleared. Mary didn't know exactly what it meant, but that was the word used: *cleared*. Like the sums you scribble in the margins of a maths exam and then rub out before submitting.

Everyone had been moved out of Digbeth and given houses in places with unusual names that Mary tried to memorise. Somehow, she could only remember the hills: Cape Hill, Sparkhill, Hodgehill, Gravelley Hill. She imagined her neighbours atop huge mounds of earth rising up beyond the horizon, like birds eating insects from the back of an elephant.

The stillness of the street was splintered by footsteps clattering along on the cobbles. Louisa, in woollen tights and a tightly wrapped turquoise scarf, approached Mary.

'What you drawing?' she asked, leaning one arm against the front door.

The question was a provocation: Mary was drawing a mermaid, and quite unmistakably so. Mermaids were an integral part of her repertoire, along with princesses, cowboys, and some of the saints. In the summer she and Louisa had drawn a whole underwater vista in chalk, using every colour in the pack. Pavement chalk was washed away by the rain or when their mother cleaned the front step, but Mary made a few sketches on the wall inside the privy that were still there, that had been embellished by other children.

The new houses all had indoor toilets, and carpets, and windows at the back. Most people had left Digbeth straight away, but the council had a deal: if you didn't like the new house, you could say no. Twice. But the third time, they'd move you whether you wanted the new house or not.

Mary's family had been offered two houses already. They'd been to see them with a man from the council whose moustache curled over his top lip and into his mouth. The first, a semi-detached house opposite a row of shops, had a window in every room and a garden each for the front and back. There was even a driveway leading up from the road. Mary assumed that it was for the milkman's float, to save him walking all the way from the pavement. After a brief tour of the house, Mary's mother had turned it down.

'Too small,' she said by way of explanation, and climbed back into the moustache's car.

The second house was in a *cul-de-sac,* which is French for dead end. The man had driven them there by turning into successively smaller roads, the route like the meandering paths of the ant farm that was kept in Mary's classroom. They exited the car and Mary's mother stood before the house, head tilted to the sky as if consulting God.

'Too quiet,' she said, and got back into the man's car before he had fished the front door key from his pocket.

On the drive back to Digbeth, he said that he would do his best to find a house that was not too small and not too quiet, but there were no guarantees – and, in fact, the remaining house might be smaller *and* quieter than either of the previous offers.

Mary's mother said nothing.

Louisa was crouched down, inspecting Mary's drawing. 'Looks like a fish,' she said.

'It's supposed to look like a fish. Half of the way, anyway.'

'I know what a mermaid looks like. *I've* seen them before.'

Mary snapped her face at Louisa. They had *both* seen a mermaid the previous summer. They were dangling their toes in the canal when they saw her swim into Typhoo Basin, turn around, and then head back out towards town, all beneath the water's glinting surface. At the time they agreed that she was staying underwater due to shyness or propriety. Since then, however, in the telling of the story Louisa had ornamented it with all sorts of details she had failed to mention at the time: the green-gold of the mermaid's eyes, the seaweed she used as a hair band, and even that she had looked at Louisa and given a slow, queenly wave.

Whenever Mary protested that those parts of the story weren't true, Louisa shrugged it off: 'You just weren't paying attention. That's why she didn't wave at you.'

Louisa was one and a bit years older. It was the *bit* that she always felt gave her a natural authority. She took one and a bit extra chips, and was one and a bit steps ahead when they danced at the St Patrick's Day festival. Even if that put her out of time with all the other girls, somehow it always looked like Mary was the one falling behind.

Mary went back to her drawing. Louisa perched behind her to get a better look.

'Her hair should be floating around her head, not falling straight down. If she's underwater.'

'I haven't decided if she's underwater yet,' said Mary without looking up.

'And you should make her more beautiful.'

'She's very beautiful. Look at her freckles.'

'And she should be singing. Mermaids are wonderful singers, I've heard them.'

Mary scoffed. 'I know what mermaids look like and what they do. I'm getting the Marina doll for Christmas.'

Louisa gave an involuntary gasp. They habitually watched *Stingray* on a neighbour's television, and were both enraptured by the mute underwater beauty who helped the submarine crew in their oceanic patrols. The end credits featured a song dedicated just to her, and it was invariably their favourite part of the show. The neighbour had moved away last month.

'No, you're not,' Louisa said at last, pretending to be casual.

'I am. I wrote a letter to Father Christmas and Mommy said he'd bring it to me if I'm a good girl,' Mary replied. She didn't need to add that she *was* a good girl – her reputation for goodness put her second or third in the whole school.

Louisa was turning red. 'He won't bring it to you. Maybe you can play with mine.'

'*You* won't have a Marina because *you* didn't ask for a Marina. He'll bring it to me down the chimney.'

Louisa's eyes darted around as she searched for a reply. 'I'm getting something much better for Christmas.'

Mary went back to her chalk. 'You just didn't know there was a Marina doll. I saw it and I wrote the letter.'

Louisa stood up and paced around in front of her sister. Mary pretended not to notice as Louisa's stomps grew faster and louder. Finally, she planted her feet apart and faced Mary like a tennis player meeting a serve.

'Father Christmas isn't real.'

Mary looked up with a knitted brow. Louisa had her arms crossed tight against her chest.

Their breaths curled in silvery clouds and trailed down the silent street, vanishing into nothing.

'What do you mean?' said Mary quietly.

'Father Christmas isn't real,' repeated Louisa, quicker than before. 'So he won't bring you a Marina down the chimney.'

Mary was gripping her chalk tighter. 'Yes, he will, I've written him a letter.'

'Your letter went in the bin,' said Louisa, gripping her arms so tightly that she seemed to be holding herself together. 'He doesn't exist.'

Mary felt her voice catch in her throat. 'No.'

'He isn't real!' spluttered Louisa. 'Your letter went in the bin, Father Christmas isn't real, and Marina isn't even a proper mermaid.'

'Yes, she is!' cried Mary, launching to her feet in outrage.

'She has legs!' Louisa shouted back, and she marched away with tightly balled fists.

Mary stood swaying, still clutching her stick of chalk. She had an urgent need to make sense of things. She opened a mental catalogue of everything she knew about Father Christmas, but couldn't bring very much to mind. He had always brought her presents. Sometimes they were not the ones she asked for, but he was a busy man. He lived at the North Pole. He was good friends with Jesus, or possibly even related.

She wanted to speak to her father, who always had a comforting reply to a question even if he didn't know the answer. But he wasn't home – instead he was at one of the other three corners of the untidy oblong that circumscribed his life: the factory where he assembled motorcycle parts, the imposing church of St. Anne, and the pub.

Her mother was in the kitchen making dinner.

Mary's mother was an atrocious cook, and it was not for want of experience. She had spent more hours than most at a stove, first as a girl and then as a woman, but they had not gifted her a knack for flavour or taste. Having children had only made things worse. A taciturn woman, she lacked the words to tell her daughters how much she loved them, so the sentiment was instead transferred to the plate. For her, a boiled vegetable was a declaration of love, and the more boiled it was the more love it declared.

Mary lingered at the kitchen doorway, swinging a leg so it would enter her mother's vision.

'What is it, Mary?' she asked, focused on the hob.

Mary gulped.

'You know Father Christmas?' she began, as if plucking the thought from the air.

With a slight cringe, her mother nodded.

'Is he…?' but the words were stuck inside Mary's belly and they would not come up. It suddenly seemed like an awful question, even an obscene one. Mary felt as she had when she laughed during a service at St Anne's. The priest had stopped speaking, and the hall filled with the sound of other worshippers turning to look her way as she buried her face in her father's sleeve.

Her mother turned to look at her. 'What's that?'

'Will he come to our new house?'

Mary's mother looked at her curiously. She wondered, as she often did, how her daughters could sound so different from her, and from her own mother, and from everybody else that she had grown up with in Kiltimagh, and how instead they had taken on this strange accent that made everything sound like a complaint. At least in Digbeth she knew everybody on the street, but now the future was an empty room, and she didn't know who would rush in to fill it.

'Of course he will,' she replied, turning back to the stove. 'Down the chimney.'

Yes, thought Mary, of course this was the answer – but it was not the right question.

'And is he real?' she asked all in one breath, the question directed at the linoleum. It stayed there on the floor for only half a moment before Mary cleared her throat and asked, 'And is Marina a proper mermaid?'

'Marina?' replied her mother, eyes on the stove. She casually consulted all the possible meanings she had for that word and couldn't make any of them fit. Mary was waiting for the answer, her eyes getting wider. 'I've got the vegetables on,' her mother said at last. 'Ask your sister.'

Mary gave a solemn nod and returned outside.

Louisa was back, fidgety and picking dried mortar from the wall. She avoided Mary's eyes.

'I just meant that Father Christmas might not find us straight away,' she said, projecting her voice.

Mary put away her stick of chalk and rubbed her foot against the pavement to clear the mermaid portrait. A smeared impression remained.

'We'll be moved by Christmas Day,' said Louisa, now looking for Mary's gaze. 'We'll have to come back and check he hasn't left the presents here by mistake.'

Mary nodded to her sister, but she knew the truth. They would never come back.

Cobbles and Cuts

RICHARD LAKIN

The rain spatters the page making the ink run. I'm sipping coffee, watching over Digbeth from above St Martin's, the church in the Bull Ring. Shoppers are sheltering. A child in sandals splashes through the puddles. Karaoke drifts from a pub lounge and a trail of strawberry vape drifts past. Digbeth has existed since Saxon times at least, but the river and the springs beneath these streets may have made it home for tribes of greater antiquity.

I need to walk off a visit to Five Guys and I want to wallow in the past. My eldest is preparing for university. I remember being that age when everything was in front of me and potential seemed limitless. Today, there's a rail strike. He's going with his girlfriend to see Kaleo at the Academy and I'm the taxi. These days I'm grateful for a few hours with nothing to do and nowhere to be. So, here I am, exploring Digbeth.

It's the late nineties and Blair is in power. There's an optimism about but it's mainly Union Jack waving and Spice Girls and seems centred on London where I'm living (if living is existing with a tin opener and microwave above an off licence). Some weekends I get the train to New Street and I walk down to the boxing club in Digbeth. I've got a mate called Tony, raised in a little bit of Italy in Perry Barr. He sells ice-cream and sorts out the marble for Italian restaurants. He coaches a bit and enjoys talking boxing, sipping coffee in vest and leather jacket, as if he's transplanted a slice of Sicily to the Pallasades.

Tony is into the psychology behind sport and greets me holding a boxing glove aloft. Just one glove, which seems odd. He says I should put my hand in it, close my eyes and meditate. I do as I'm told but I don't know what to think while I make a fist as if I'm going to land a right hook. I get a funny look from the old dear beside us in Druckers as she pauses in buttering her scone. Tony says it was Sugar Ray Leonard's glove and the magic will wear off on me. I close my eyes and decide to believe. That afternoon I get a black eye and a split lip in sparring. I guess it's another Ray Leonard who owned it, one from Stirchley perhaps.

I'm doing a lot of boxing training and my girlfriend is living in Gravelly Hill so, depending on cash, I'm travelling back and forth to Digbeth coach station or New Street rather a lot. Getting in from London I visibly relax, shoulders dropping an inch as people hold doors, call me 'bab' and don't bawl me out for standing on the left on an escalator. New Street was darker then, a subterranean concrete bunker with occasional glimpses of skies above. I dash past left luggage, the Transport Police, and the choking fumes of the taxi rank and head downwards, always downwards.

It was the old Bull Ring then — the Sixties shopping centre and market (you can still marvel at in its full splendour on YouTube). I descend through the concrete underpass, weaving between market stalls and dribbling scattered veg around pavement cracks or scoring a penalty with a dropped onion, until I climb the ramp past the Ship Ashore pub and turn for Digbeth. I have a spring in my step here, daring to try a few moves if I'm not being watched, inspired by Birmingham's benches, ramps, and staircases.

Digbeth lies on the crossing over the river Rea. Yes, Birmingham has a river. The city centre rests on a plateau, the landscape and rainwater falling away through the factories, pubs, and streets, so the contours deprive New Street and Colmore Row of a waterfront. Birmingham's river is a shy one. It's not large and it's tucked away in brick culverts, often buried, or trickling between knotweed, graffitied brick and factory wall. It will be gushing like a Welsh mountain stream with this unexpected downpour. Beneath Digbeth there are springs too. Fresh water that would've fed the early settlement and then heavy industry.

Twenty-five years and more have passed. I married my girlfriend from Scotland via Gravelly Hill and have long since hung up my gloves. Digbeth isn't celebrated by psychogeographers or travel writers, but there's a lot to see for those prepared to explore and I've memories to rekindle. I've no set agenda or specific route to take, just a stroll through the streets, taking in the new artwork or old haunts and secrets. The pleasure in visiting an unheralded district is that there's much to discover. I often walk London too, with notebook and phone, and there are always secrets and new discoveries, but unlike B5, so much of our capital has already been photographed, videoed, sketched or painted or sung about.

It's a walk I've done hundreds of times: as a student; boxing at Birmingham City; as a reporter; as a police officer; in a drunken stagger home at closing time; running for a bus; or jogging down to the Stratford Road. Years later, at lunchtimes, I'd escape the office at nearby Priestley Wharf, leaving my suit jacket slung on a chair and loosening my tie to head for the Cut and Digbeth. I'd throw a pebble at a bottle bobbing in the murky waters and stride beneath the railway, shuffling to avoid pigeons and towpath cyclists, as I munched on a sandwich. It was a brief escape from monthly meetings, TM Lewin ties and shouty emails, but a glance at the oily waters of the Digbeth Branch Canal and thoughts of doing a Reggie Perrin never lingered.

Here was a crisscross of lines: canal and railway and ancient tracks and roads; over and under. It always brought to mind the comics of my childhood – *Whizzer and Chips* and *Buster* and, in particular X-Ray Specs: the boy whose amazing glasses meant he could see through anything. If I could be X-Ray Specs what could I see beneath these streets? Maybe the odd Saxon sword from Beorma's reign, sacred objects left by Celts at the springs, but far more likely the broken, rusting machines and tools of a hundred workshops. Nails and screws and hooks and the metal kind of spring, perhaps. There would be pipes and tunnels and cables and streams and foundations of ancient buildings; the legacy of heavy industry; old roads and tracks, bridleways, and desire paths; evidence of fire and flood; and still – at least for the few not dug up and moved for HS2 – the graves of our ancestors. The city was a workshop for the world and the forefathers of many modern-day Brummies packed up what they could carry and walked into it in search of work. They hoped, as people still do, for a better life. Not to be hungry or cold.

In BBC's *HS2 – The Biggest Dig*, Professor Alice Roberts had access to the site where the new Curzon Street high-speed rail station is being built. Many of these skeletons would be people who lived and worked in Digbeth and the surrounding streets. Some would be the rural poor, their lives changed immeasurably in just a few months from backbreaking toil in the wet fields of the surrounding shires to the danger and drudgery and long hours of factories and workshops. Many of these people were buried in Park Street when there were no plots left at St Martin's, where our walk began.

Thousands of skeletons were removed to be re-interred, many deformed with rickets and other illnesses, or killed in industrial accidents. Most intriguing, perhaps, were the ones buried with plates of salt clutched to their chest. This was believed to protect the immortal spirit – a clear demonstration of the myths and folklore the first generations of rural folk brought with them and held dear. The ways of the country – the fireside stories and long, dark nights – must've clashed with the science and reason of industry. What must this change have been like for families who laboured over the same few acres for centuries? Lives set by daybreak and sunset, the patterns of the harvests and seasons, would never be the same for them again.

Now Birmingham is changing again, awakening perhaps, or at least realising it has an important role to play and shake off the lazy prejudice it has suffered for so long. Maybe Birmingham's shrug of the shoulders can be considered an asset. It doesn't do swagger or glam much and doesn't need to see itself as a rival to London or other cities, or as its own little republic. Its people are down to earth, friendly, and straight talking. Birmingham has welcomed generations of migrants – those walking into the city from the hamlets of Staffordshire or Worcestershire, the Welsh and the Irish, people who came from China, the Caribbean, India, and Pakistan, and more recently across Europe.

The rain is finally giving way. I make my way down the steps. I head away from the stalls selling basketball boots, sweaters, watches and veg, and pause outside the Bull Ring Tavern. It sounds as if it's rocking inside. I take a peek and see a woman singing Shania Twain egged on by a few regulars sipping pints of cider. She wears a silver glittery cowboy hat and she's giving it maximum effort, crouching, and throwing a few karate kicks, letting a fella at the bar in cut-off denims know he don't impress her much.

The ancient parish of Digbeth has been dug up, but it's highways not archaeologists with the shovels, so I'm stuck on the west side of the road. There are cones and fences everywhere and barely a place to cross unless you've got wire cutters or grappling hooks and rope. What an odd raggle-taggle blend of businesses Digbeth offers. You could say it's Birmingham's Kings Cross, but that wouldn't be accurate. Yes, Digbeth is called the Cultural Quarter, but it is still industrial. It hasn't given itself over to coffee served via chemistry sets (at this end at least). Instead, it hammers metal, spray-paints cars, welds girders, collects skips, runs minicabs, and provides security. A typical run of businesses is sex shop, sandwich shop, chicken shop, lockups, old men's boozers, taxi firms, college, gyms, and off licences. I pass signs for karate lessons – perhaps Digbeth's answer to Shania Twain does her kata here – and gaming workshops and language lessons (although it doesn't specify which language). I pass the National Express coach station, memories of lugging rucksacks and assorted nick-nacks from bedsit to flat to student halls in my distant past. Across the road is the Kerryman where Irish granddads would totter out in Celtic or Blues colours after a few pints. It brings flashbacks passing Milk Street and Meriden Street. I'd pause here for a glance in Sparky's Magic Piano, or the drinkers at the Bull's Head. I'm glad to see the pub's still busy despite being almost entirely fenced in by the roadworks.

In an age when ghost signs are being appreciated again with dedicated social media sites, I see an ad on a wall in Milk Street for *Melox Marvels – The Healthy Biscuits for Dogs*. It's a Victorian survivor from an era when these streets supplied an empire. Typhoo tea and Bird's custard. The Custard Factory is home to those working in the creative industries, while the BBC has recently announced a move to nearby Typhoo Wharf.

Just along the road beyond some railings, tucked away in a yard was Birmingham City Boxing Club. It's moved along the

Stratford Road now but was once here in Digbeth. Frank O'Sullivan MBE has coached scores of champions. It was a proper old-school gym in an industrial unit, with a worn canvas ring, scalding showers and bags creaking from the iron girders that supported the factory roof. Pro fighters like Rob McCracken came here to train and learn and Michael Flatley, of Riverdance fame, was said to have popped in one day to show off his footwork and spar a few rounds. It's no coincidence the Lord of the Dance visited Digbeth, which has always had strong Irish links. The St Patrick's Day Parade takes place here – the largest in England. Birmingham's Irish Centre was just across the road and there's a mural to JFK, commissioned by the Irish community, which stands nearby.

The streets here are full of factories, workshops, and units. The odd pub or sandwich bar is tucked away, surviving post-Covid to feed hungry mechanics, spray-painters, welders, and poets. Yes, writers and artists get hungry too, and the Custard Factory is a lively hub of creatives. The river Rea rushes along its brick channels, beneath us, culverted or between factory walls. It can flash flood in heavy rain and its course is charted by debris and graffiti that rises from the unofficial tags of the brick-lined channels to the commissioned work on the railway arches leading into the Custard Factory. The river can be seen and heard here but is often out of sight, though there are always clues to its presence. There is the obvious River Street and Rea Street, and Floodgate gives its name to a street, a bar, and studios.

In River Street I pass a unit with its metal roller door pulled down, but the thud of a snare drum and pluck of a bass guitar rattles the steel shutters. Heavy metal is rooted in the Midlands, with a strong heritage in these streets. Among the numerous artworks portrayed on the red brick and concrete of Digbeth is a Black Sabbath mural. Digbeth has its own walking tour of murals and artwork. It is ever-changing.

Digbeth, according to Wiki at least, could be derived from 'dig-path' or 'duck's bath' but I much prefer the unlikely explanation from the coming of industry: that the air pollution of the era led to it being called 'dragon's breath.' It's a suggestion likely to please the band rehearsing behind the roller shutters.

The Cut and the railway, the main roads Dr Johnson and perhaps Shakespeare may have walked seem immovable, but the creases and contours of this district and its neighbouring streets are always changing. You can watch from the London or Coventry train above, or the glass viewing holes in the huge hoardings surrounding the HS2 site. Oddly, you can see the headstones and cobbled streets of precisely this spot – ghost images of a few years' past – and a family getting out of a taxi, seemingly frozen forever on Google Street View. Some buildings in Digbeth become rubble, others like the Old Crown pub, exist for centuries. Fashions change but faces hardly seem to. They drink and they laugh and they cry and they dance and they kiss. They're a forever presence – locked in Street View or black-and-white images or bones in the soil or dropped hatpins or coins – timeless and in transit like the Rea and the Cut and the railway.

The Things We Once Held True

ALAN KANE FRASER

Friday night was Metal Night at the Barrel Organ. The night when one corner of Digbeth became a roiling sea of long hair, black leather and denim. The people who went to Metal Night weren't the cool ones you might find at the Rum Runner or Tressines, but they formed a very distinct tribe of their own which over time I found myself joining. Coming from Handsworth, being an outcast felt natural to me, so I was never worried that we were called 'Greasers' and thought to be dirty by all the Duranees and 'Frankie-Says-Relax' wannabees.

Over the course of my final year in sixth form, Friday nights at the Barrel Organ became a focal point in my diary. Every week I'd get the 74 into town with Baby Dave and then we'd head down the back of the station and along the High St, joining as we did so a thin line of black that trickled through Digbeth like ants. There was something about that walk that struck me, even then. The faded splendour of the old Victorian warehouses hinted at a great and glorious commercial past for the city that the newer buildings suggested had now been lost. Even as Baby Dave would talk animatedly about Dio and Motörhead, there was something in me that wanted to know why. Why was it that the building which housed the Barrel Organ, which I guessed had been around for no more than thirty years, looked worse than the police station opposite which had stood for more than seventy?

Once we reached the Barrel Organ though, all that would be forgotten. We'd meet the other guys from school – some combination of Ricky, Sanjay, Tall Paul, Fat Phil and Nello. Nello would usually bring his girlfriend, Dee, too. He was the only one of us with a girlfriend and I noticed that her presence would change the dynamics of the group; there was none of the sniggering and chest puffing you got when she wasn't there.

At school they called her Freaky Dee because she wore heavy black eyeliner, listened to Iron Maiden, and didn't want to snog George Michael. But to us she was just Dee, and her presence made us feel — and behave — like we were more grown up. Dee had jet black, back-combed hair that fell over her black-lined eyes in a way that made her look a bit like Siouxsie Sioux. There was a lot we disagreed about as a group but the two things we all agreed on were a) that *No Sleep 'til Hammersmith* was the greatest 'live' album of all time and b) that Dee was beautiful. Being her boyfriend gave Nello a strange authority over the rest of us that he hadn't had before he started dating her. We would all sit in marvelled awe of him and wonder at how he'd managed to capture her heart.

Of course, one of the big attractions of Nello — for all of us, but especially, we suspected, for Dee — was that Nello knew Skeetch.

Skeetch was a short, muscly guy, with close-cropped salt-and-pepper hair and a receding hairline. He seemed impossibly old to us then but looking back I guess he must only have been mid-to-late forties. He wore a sleeveless denim jacket over his leather with the insignia of the HAMC Oakland chapter on it. This led some people to conclude that Skeetch was a Hell's Angel. But no one ever saw him on a motorbike or in the presence of any other Angels, so the story started going round that he was ex-special forces, and the jacket was a cover he'd used for a Black Ops assignment. But Tall Paul's dad had been in the Army, and he said that was ridiculous. Sanjay was insistent that he'd overheard one of the doormen say that the jacket was a trophy Skeetch had taken off a man he'd killed in a bar fight. But nobody really knew and Skeetch didn't seem interested in enlightening us.

The one thing we did know for sure about Skeetch though, was that he was the Barrel Organ's resident drug dealer. This was not an officially remunerated position, and it certainly wasn't recognised by the Barrel Organ's management, who maintained a close relationship with the police station over the road to try and keep dealing off their premises. Consequently, Skeetch was obliged to undertake his activities discretely. So, whilst everybody at the Barrel Organ knew *of* Skeetch, only a select few knew him well enough to actually buy off him. If anyone he didn't know approached him trying to buy, he'd just blank them or mutter darkly, 'I think you've got the wrong guy. I dunno what you're talking about.'

That was why Nello had to act as our buyer. No one could work out how Nello had got to know Skeetch, and Nello would never explain. Like the precise details of Skeetch's involvement in the Hell's Angels, the mystery around the issue only added to the aura around the person. Nello knew this and played on it. I came to think it was what Dee loved about him.

The upshot of this was that every Friday we'd all chip in a couple of quid and Nello would buy an eighth off Skeetch. Dee would roll a couple of joints for us – she was the only one of us who could consistently roll a decent four-skin joint – and whatever dope was left after she'd done that was handed over to her, ostensibly as payment for her joint-rolling skills. Impressive as these undoubtedly were, in retrospect, this was a spectacularly good deal for Dee and an extremely poor one for the rest of us. As with

Digbeth's old buildings however, we favoured beauty over utility and Dee's beauty exerted a strange hold over us, which caused us to suspend the critical judgments that our more rational minds might otherwise have reached.

The routine of those Friday evenings generally never varied. Most of them, therefore, have melded into a single combined memory for me with nothing to distinguish one from all the others.

But there's one Friday I won't forget: the night I got to meet Skeetch face-to-face. The funny thing is, that wasn't the most memorable thing about it.

Up until closing time everything proceeded as usual. Then, the usual routine was for Nello to catch Skeetch's eye and follow him out to a rendezvous point round the corner where the aforesaid transaction would take place away from the prying eyes of the Barrel Organ's doormen. We'd then find a spot at the back of the coach station to smoke our joints before walking back towards town, getting chips at Mr Egg and the night bus home. But on this particular night, as we made our way to the Barrel Organ's exit, some guy started trying to chat up Dee and Nello decided to intervene. He assumed the problem was that the guy didn't realise Dee was with him and that once he did, he would just back off. But it turned out that wasn't the problem at all. The problem was the guy had been drinking and this had led him to conclude that he was better option for Dee than Nello was. As a consequence, Nello found himself an unwilling participant in a fight which quickly got out of hand and had to be broken up by the doormen. Nello and the guy were both thrown out.

The first rule of scoring off Skeetch was that that buyers had to meet him alone, but after the fight Nello was worried that the drunk guy might come back and jump him, so he asked us to come round the corner with him. The mood had changed though, and Tall Paul and Ricky had seen enough. They stood the loss on the money they'd handed over and headed home. Fat Phil hadn't come out that night so that left me, Sanjay and Baby Dave to act as guards.

Sanjay and Baby Dave guarded Dee whilst also acting as lookouts. Meanwhile Nello took me with him to meet Skeetch. We were both nervous because of what had happened and that, along with the fact that Nello had broken Skeetch's golden rule, put Skeetch on edge. There was always a haunted look about him that I guess comes with spending your entire life trying to hide what you're doing. But that night it was something more.

As the two of us approached I saw Skeetch's eyes narrow. He had the kind of pained, distrusting eyes that suggested he was silently judging us.

'What's up?' His voice was low and menacing, like the tread of an intruder on a carpeted hallway.

'Nothing, I promise,' said Nello. 'I just had a bit of a run-in with a guy. It's nothing you need to worry about, Skeetch. Honest. You know me. We're good, man. I swear we're good.'

Skeetch looked at Nello, as though searching him for a truth that was hiding behind what he was actually saying. 'Who was the guy? What did he want?'

'Nothing, man. It was just girl trouble, y'know? It was nothing to do with you. I promise. I just felt like I needed some protection though. In case he came back.'

Skeetch's attention transferred to me. His look seemed to bore into me, and I found myself rooted to the spot. The idea that he might have killed a man in a bar fight suddenly felt like more than just a fanciful story.

'This is Jake,' Nello said by way of explanation. 'He's solid, I promise. Just protection for me. No worries, man. No worries.'

Nello got our money out and handed it over to Skeetch, who took it from him guardedly and checked it. Skeetch's eyes flicked between the two of us. Up until that point no crime had been committed, but the moment he handed over the eighth he was breaking the law. So if there was a less innocent explanation for Nello's uncharacteristic nervousness and my presence, then that was the point at which he would incriminate himself. Which I guess is why he paused.

He looked at us; we looked at him.

The world seemed to freeze for a moment.

Then we heard Baby Dave shout from behind us: 'Fuck! He's back – with his mates. Fuckin' run!'

I saw Baby Dave and Sanjay race past me towards the relative safety of the coach station and then felt Nello push past me to try and make it there too. A second later, a group of about half-a-dozen guys, led by the guy from the pub, tore round the corner and ran after them.

I expected Skeetch to bolt too. But he stood rock solid and didn't move. At first, I couldn't understand why, but then it slowly dawned on me: to run would make him look guilty of something. And if this was a police sting then they would have officers on every available escape route anyway. He'd only be running into their arms and the simple fact of his running would give them probable cause to search him. But to stand still when everyone else is running makes you look like an innocent bystander. Which, of course, he was.

I wanted to run too, to join Baby Dave, Sanjay and Nello in the coach station. But there was something about the way that Skeetch fixed me with his stare that rendered me immobile. For what felt like an age we just stood there, staring at each other; Skeetch apparently unwilling to take his gaze off from me, and me finding myself unable to take mine off him. I felt my heart beating like a fucked clock and a wave of nausea rise up in my stomach as my heart sank to meet it.

Eventually, when Skeetch was satisfied that no police were coming, he broke the tableau.

'Well, your friend has paid for this, so I suppose you'd better have it.'

And with that he dropped a small block of cellophane-wrapped dope into my hand, turned on his heels and disappeared into the night.

'Jake! Jake! Are you alright?'

I turned to see Dee standing on the corner, shaking.

'Yeah, I'm fine,' I said. 'What about you?'

'Fuckin' wrecked. I just want to get out of here.' She was the year below us at school, but because of her figure and eyeliner could generally pass as early-twenties. In that moment though, she looked every inch the frightened teenager.

'We should go into the coach station and try and find the others,' I said.

'Are you kiddin' me? We don't know what's going on in there. And that nutter is looking for me. We need to get *away* from here before he comes back.'

Despite my sense of loyalty to my friends, it occurred to me that she was right. Nello had Sanjay and Baby Dave to look after him. It was my job to protect Dee. I couldn't fight off a group of guys spoiling for a fight, so the only sensible course of action was for me and Dee to get out of there as soon as possible.

Dee's older brother worked the bar at the Irish Centre and would always take her home after Metal Night so she didn't have to take the night bus. It was early April, and the temperature was dropping fast, so I took off my leather jacket and draped it over her shoulders. Then we rejoined the main road through Digbeth and set off towards the Irish Centre.

'Christ, I need a joint just to calm me down,' she said. 'Did you get that eighth?'

I handed it over and Dee rolled up a joint in double quick time. We smoked it between us unhurriedly and the whole night began to slow down.

We stopped opposite Digbeth Civic Hall to finish the joint before we reached the Irish Centre. Despite the traffic and the drunken revellers and the police vans tearing up and down, the hit from the dope made Digbeth seem strangely peaceful. People could say what they liked about Skeetch, but he never sold you shit. His stuff always got you mellow.

It was then that I began to notice the buildings again. I generally never walked as far down as the Civic Hall, so I'd never really looked at it before. But there it was; an Arts and Crafts building in the middle of what used to be a slum.

'Isn't that a beautiful building?' I said. 'What it's doing here?'

'My nan says it used to be a church.'

'A church?' I turned to look at her quizzically. 'Are you sure? Doesn't look like a church.'

'Well, it was *built* by a church – the one on Carrs Lane, I think. I don't think they held services here. But they'd do lectures and stuff. Educate the poor, y'know? My nan used to get brought here. She only lived down the road. Always said the Institute was the prettiest building in Digbeth.'

'The Institute?'

'Yeah, it was called the Digbeth Institute back then, but then the Council bought it.'

My dope-fogged mind looked at the building in front of me. A question arose in my mind that I couldn't shake. 'Why'd they bother, d'you think?'

'Why'd the Council buy it? I dunno. Probably just wanted to stop it getting knocked down.'

That wasn't what I'd meant. What I'd meant was why had the church bothered to make it look beautiful? The Irish Centre, just a few feet away, was basically a rectangular metal box with a hole cut in the front for the entrance. It wasn't pretty, but it was probably cheaper to build and maintain.

But actually, Dee's question was a good one too. Why *had* the Council bought it? Why hadn't they just let it be knocked down? Plenty of buildings in Digbeth had been and it was difficult to imagine the Council buying the Irish Centre – or even the Barrel Organ – in order to preserve them for future generations.

I was heavily stoned, so this was not a question I felt able to answer. All I knew was that, for all the neglect that it had been subjected to, the Civic Hall seemed to promise a different kind of world to the one that surrounded me. Maybe that's why it had taken a church to build something like the Civic Hall, or the Institute, or whatever it was called. Maybe you needed to believe in something in order to see the point in creating something beautiful.

The idea grew within me that everyone in Birmingham should be like the people in that church. They believed in beauty, and I wanted a city that believed the future should be beautiful, even in places like Digbeth. Somewhere along the way we'd stopped believing that. Or maybe we'd just stopped believing that Birmingham deserved it. I couldn't make any sense of it. But in that moment, something in me wanted to reach out and hug that building, just as much as I wanted to have a girlfriend like Dee who I could reach out and hug. I decided that was what I needed for happiness. It felt then that it was all I needed for happiness, although I guess I know better now.

I felt my arm reach out involuntarily; maybe to Dee, maybe to the building, I couldn't tell which.

'Come on,' said Dee, pulling away from me. 'My brother will be out soon.' And she turned and headed up towards the entrance of the Irish Centre.

The moment, if that's what it had been, had gone. I remember regretting that and I remember feeling guilty that I did. Nello was my mate.

'I hope Nello's alright,' I said, following on behind her.

'Yeah,' she said. 'I hope so too. I hate it when that kind of shit happens.'

'Ugly business,' I said.

'Yeah. That kind of ugliness spoils everything.'

In Search of a Workable Title

SARAH SPILSBURY

Hilary wandered from his flat in a vague state of discombobulation. Part of this was due to not being used to waking up in Birmingham. Another was due to having slept poorly without his usual (generous) nightcap.

He entered the Custard Factory and found the designated office. Thank Christ he wasn't hanging: everything was so white – most days it would have burnt his retinas, even through, or perhaps exacerbated, by his glasses.

He sat at a white desk, firing up his pretty much white Apple, on a white table, in a white room, inside a large white building. This was like being in the video for 'Imagine'! Total stain-hazard: John and Yoko's décor would soon have been messed up if they'd had Hilary's red wine habit.

Or was this more a whiteness that could only have been imagined in the most fervid dreams of Mosley, Powell, or more recently Farage?

But race relations wasn't part of Hilary's remit (yet, or at least he hoped not). He sat and fired up the lappy to read the ideas of the people he was there to represent, trying to get his head round their brain-frying lollapalooza of art world buzz words.

So essentially the oeuvre of the artiste's work is the subversion of notions of reality, bringing historical artefacts into the current zeitgeist, to confound the expectations of the viewer in a way reminiscent of the situationist movement, but with a retro neo-futuristic slant, with a nod being paid to the concept of homage to the Russian Constructivist movement, employing guerrilla art tactics.

Hilary scanned over what he had typed. Did the description really sufficiently hype up this collection of photographs of what looked a hell of a lot like fly postings for Franz Ferdinand? Two-tone stencilled pictures of 1930's domestic settings with cryptic slogans. He was sure it was very worthy. He was sure that the *artiste* in question (their word not his — who was he to query these NBA types?) had put quite considerable thought into this project.

What he wasn't sure of was whether or not it was any good.

But who the hell was he to raise questions? Despite the requisite vision, he had long been forced to admit that, in the artistic world, he had only the talent to carry out the administrative side of things. Acting as the midwife was as good as he was going to get. His true artistry fell within the sector of the promoter, the publicist, the gabby fucker whose job it was to divert the art-enjoying (and enduring) public's attention from the fact that the Emperor was not even wearing last season's clothes.

These photographs represent a work in progress of Black Country maverick outfit, FOUND MESS-AGE. From ground level, apparently random assemblages appearing to be found in situ, only revealing their true communicative intention when viewed from above...

Great! So now the world could share in what had previously been a well-kept secret, jealously guarded by people riding high rise trains, unlikely literate birds, and those of an unusually lofty stature. Because let's face facts: there was no point shouting about a bunch of bricks shaped to form the message *I love you*, unless of course, you were pimping and priming them for an exhibition such as this.

These works bring the Japanese concept of obos into an utterly British setting.

And, thanks to the aerial-only usual viewing opportunities, were about as easily understood as Japanese.

The content of the next set of offerings was equally banal, once you took the one-laugh joke out of it. Someone had taken a series of photographs of various messages written in chalk on a wall. They gave little snippets of information about the day, Facebook style, only on a literal wall. Really, what was the art world coming to?

The fact that the next set of work he was required to write up on involved paint was no redeemer, seeing as all it was used for was signwriting of pseudo-provocative phrasing.

What are you thinking now? read one.

I'm thinking that you must have taken to art as a last-ditch refuge, unable to find anyone who wanted their shop front done by you. On account of your shite lack of talent.

But he wasn't going to say this.

He couldn't: these were 'Tony's cronies' – just as sinister in their takeover of the Birmingham art world as Blair's had been on a larger scale. Unlike Alastair Campbell, Hilary's spin and huckstering was unlikely to lead to being branded a war criminal.

'Hmmmm…' He found himself chewing on the end of his biro and hoped no one else had been at it in the office before him.

Artisan techniques employed to convey a contemporary message?

Or might that be better for the chalk wall? He could make a pun from con-temporary, given their wash-away nature…

Neo-something?

Everything, thanks to post-modernity making everything a repeat of repetition, was, by default, 'neo'-something-or-other.

Neo-shite!

Neo-crass-art-wank!

Neo-neo-no-doubt-nepotism!

Neo… neuralgia?

Well, the signage had given him a headache.

Neo-necrophilia?

Nah…leave that for *Bizarre* magazine…

Well, whatever neon neo-ness Hilary was going to pull out of the bag, he was going to have to produce it pretty niftily as the publicity for the private view was due to hit the social media networks tomorrow. He had no intention of replicating Peter Saville, who had brought the publicity posters for the first of Factory Records club nights, at the end of said night, rendering them beautiful, if useless, memorabilia… even though this made Saville more legendary than countless others who had delivered the goods on time. He did toy with making a memorable muck up to seal his name in notoriety but decided that it would only go against him whilst he was trying to make a good impression.

Neo-phyte?

After all, they were all newbies.

Nah: neophyte newbies doesn't cut it.…Non-entities?

Accurate, but unflattering.

Neophyte notables? Aha! Neo Now!

He paced about, snapping his fingers as he tried it out for size: 'Neo! Now! New! Happening! Schwing!'

'Hey! Hilary, my main man! Are you presenting with some ideas?'

Speak of the devil.

Today the devil (who used the name Julian on official documentation) was wearing shades, a fishing hat and a flack-jacket. Had he been watching *Fear and Loathing in Las Vegas*? Or still thinking that Ocean Colour Scene were ambassadors of cool, rather than the fag end of Weller-worship that had dogged Br*t-p*p? Hilary put the asterixis in, mentally. It had all been a bit too flag-wavey, in the end, hadn't it? People had innocently assumed 'National Front Disco' had been Morrissey displaying a warped sense of humour, rather than a precursor to owning his back catalogue becoming 'politically problematic.'

'Just tossing off titles.'

Very apposite, for a pile of wanky gewgaws.

'So what are you bringing to the table?'

'Neo Now?' Hilary blundered into the trap of making the proposition sound like a question. Like he was Australian? Or a young person? He shuddered at the self-recognition.

'Hold that thought.' Julian pointed towards him, as Hilary had a mental image of himself catching an assortment of literal thought bubbles in his arms. 'Let me give you a steer. That's good, it's edgy, but I'm not quite sure it nails what we're looking for. I don't know if 'Neo Now' is going to capture the imagination of the Birmingham art-going public.'

There was one? Where had they been shipped in from? Precisely how many people lived in Moseley?

'We really need to think outside the box on this one…'

In which case, couldn't Julian have given him a better example than a gut-churningly cheesy cliché?

'Big ask, I know, but any chance you can come up with an alternative? And hey, keep me in the loop with this, yes?' No sooner had he arrived, the new-speak-wank-mouth-Arts-equivalent-of-David-Brent announced he was disappearing into one of the neighbouring offices, to no doubt jibber-jabber in similar on-trend jargon with similar minded, linguistically perverted types, on yet another round of Funded Arts Bullshit Bingo.

Hilary cleared his throat. 'Yes, Julian. Will do.'

Christ, he was too old for all this. He had nothing against blinding people with a bit of vertiginous hyperbole, bloviation, and sesquipedalia, but this constant barrage of babble was something else. He considered the other things he still had to fix up: confirming the room booking, arranging hangings ('Very Pierrepoint'), continuing the 'conversations' with the submitters regarding their statements – and then the inevitable strops and sulks he would have to try and pave over when he failed to understand their 'visions'.

And that was prior to the most important part of the opening private view: arranging suitably smart snacks and squiffy-juice.

After checking his email — Lovett Gough was already splitting hairs re: the semantics of his statement. What the hell was the bloody difference between 'articulate' and 'communicate' anyhow? And who'd been the journalist round here? — Hilary sighed, fired off a few more electronic missives, and settled his mind. He was going to test run a few of the suggestions for the wine. Not out of a sense of duty (although this was the rationale he sold himself) but because he bloody well felt the need for a stiff one — a stiff cock would have been welcome but the wine was more readily available.

And cheaper.

A few glasses in from the assortment, Hilary was no better off. His tastebuds were now simply confused, although attuned and ready for the next offering. He mused on his predicament. How had it come to the present moment, him slumped on the sofa in a scantily furnished studio flat, with only wine to keep him warm, worrying about some no-hope back street art outfit? He thought of the self-questioning lyrics from 'Once In A Lifetime'.

'And you may ask yourself,' he continued, playing auteur with the Talking Heads, 'Why do I do it? Hmmm. Why do I do it?' He took another slurp of something Chilean and red. 'I do it for Art!'

He had to giggle: it was preposterous.

But maybe that was what was required.

'I Do It For Art… *We* Do It For Art? *THEY* Do It For Art! Hmm – well what other bucking reason they do it for I don't know…'

Had he stumbled on that elusive unicorn, a workable title?

In the Blood

NIGEL PROCTOR

Charlie-Boy was not having the best of evenings and now he's going to end the night missing at least one knee cap.

Definitely one, probably both.

Charlie-Boy's assailants stand over him as a flash flood of urine soaks the inside thigh of his grubby chinos. He is nothing to them. Maybe even someone to feel sorry for, given different circumstances, given a different life lived.

Joe speaks first. 'So, what you reckon?'

Colin looks over. 'Depends.'

'Depends?'

'Depends on the level of resistance we encounter.'

Smooth with the words, Colin can talk the talk and when you need someone to walk the walk, he is the one and only – at least in Joe's eyes.

'Yeah?'

'Most certainly.'

'So what say we start with the hammer, you know, get it going, like? And then, maybe, finish with the cutters?'

Colin smiles back. 'Sounds about right to me. It has a certain balance. The proper yinyang.'

Yinyang? Is that some sort of Chinese gang thing? Colin is right up on his Chinese stuff, so chances are it is. Joe, not wanting to seem stupid, nods and speaks: 'Sounds good, you be yin and I'll be yang.'

Colin laughs and Joe watches as a hammer head smashes a human knee.

Blood joins urine.

Passing out, Charlie-Boy hears a distant scream that couldn't possibly belong to him. It just couldn't.

The screaming stops.

'He's passed out.'

'You don't say?'

Joe bends in close to Charlie-Boy, slaps a cheek.

Charlie-Boy opens a snot-stained eye – it looks more like a semi-shucked oyster – and groans. Driven by instinct and nothing else, he rolls over and starts to drag himself away, leaving a snail's trail of blood and cartilage behind him.

His assailants, half-amused, half-disturbed, watch his efforts and then in six strides, Colin catches up with him. 'And where do you think you're going?'

Colin raises his hands in front of him. He's discarded the sledgehammer and now holds a slim set of industrial bolt cutters. He opens them once and closes them with a snick. 'I think it's time we addressed the matter of your sticky fingers in a more direct manner. What do you say, Joe?'

But the ground has opened up and Joe is gone.

Who was it who'd suggested the old warehouse? You know, the one on the Grand Union? That one. The one through the arches. That old knacker of a building with the big metal balcony and half its roof missing.

Dirty old place.

Scary old place, with creaking iron gates and oil-stained stone, a stone which seemed to swallow shadows. Haunted, they say – no, really, proper haunted – haven't you never heard the stories?

Still, didn't matter, not really — who cared who'd suggested it? The old warehouse is the perfect place to settle a bit of business. Only this bit of business is not going perfect.

Sure, finding Charlie-Boy had been easy enough. Always was. Very reliable, Charlie-Boy. Any time he had disposable cash you could guarantee he'd stick it straight up his nose and that's what he'd done. Thing is, it wasn't his cash to dispose of in the first place.

Chasing him down was like chasing the dragon in a coal hole. Check out a few pubs and bars in and around Digbeth or tap up his favoured dealer — no, that's wrong: tap up the only dealer who'd still do business with him — and there, or thereabouts, you'd find Charlie-Boy.

And that's what they'd done. And that's where he'd been. And then they'd brought him here.

But now Joe is somewhere else, flat on his back, staring up at the night sky. The sky framed by the hole in the floor through which he'd just fallen. A hole which, in turn, is framed by a hole in the warehouse roof.

Joe remembers seeing Colin bound over to Charlie-Boy, cutters in hand, and he remembers stooping down to pick up the discarded sledgehammer. The head of the hammer had sunk into the wooden floor — gone proper deep into rotten boards — and as Joe struggles to pull it free, the planking under his feet sags and he plunges down into darkness.

Plunges down too quick to cry out.

Joe isn't sure but nothing feels broken. He moves his fingers and then his arms. Everything seems to be working.

And then his legs. Yeah, no problem there, either.

His neck hurts a bit but it don't seem nothing serious.

As his vision adjusts, Joe sees that the canal side wall is a run of stone columns and alcoves. Each alcove dark and deep like the dilated pupil of an enormous eye, staring at him, staring into him.

Or worse still, a hungry maw, open wide in anticipation of being fed.

He shivers and his head starts to hurt.

There's a cruiserweight headache incoming — a Christ-awful combination of drink and drugs, both wearing off at the same time. Fuck, he can't be having with this, any of this. Fumbling in a trouser pocket, he pulls out a cellophane baggy.

Lioresal.

He shovels four pills into his mouth, chews, swallows, waits for the pain to dull and the world blur around the edges.

For the eyes to look away.

The mouths to close.

Colin jabs Charlie-Boy in the ribs with the cutters. 'Don't move, right? Don't you move, or you won't know what hit you, yeah?'

Charlie-Boy grunts: he isn't sure he could move.

Isn't sure he'll ever move again.

Colin walks towards where he'd last seen Joe, peers down and through the perished boards. 'Joe? Are you there, Joe?'

'Yeah, I'm here.' A dry, dusty whisper from a lost place.

Colin pulls a small torch from a pocket. Rotating the end of the barrel, he points the light down into the hole. It barely touches the dark. 'Joe?'

'Yeah?'

'Where are you?'

'I'm over here.'

Colin widens the beam, leans forward, pans the torch from side to side. The floor under his feet creaks and cracks.

Unlike Joe, Colin lands on something soft.

He lands on Joe.

Joe explodes like a burst party balloon and throws Colin aside. 'Christ.'

Colin stands, fumbles for his torch, points it at his friend.

The overspill picks out the back wall.

'Shit,' Colin says.

'What?' Joe inhales hard and sits up. 'What? What is it?'

What had been the doorway is bricked in.

Joe groans. 'Fuck sake.'

Colin shines his torch around the room, lights up a second door in the opposite wall. 'Now, that is kind of interesting.'

'What is?

'That is.'

Colin walks over. The door looks like an old bank vault. He spins the large central wheel. It moves. He tugs at it. The door gives an inch. 'Lend us a hand here, will you?'

A minute later, the door is fully open.

Darkness within darkness.

More stomach-churning malodour.

Joe winces. 'And I thought out here smelled bad.'

'It does, it's just in there smells worse.' Colin steps forward, sniffs the air. 'That is not a life-enhancing aroma.'

Colin takes another step. Joe holds back, uncertain. 'And you want to go in?'

'I'm not seeing any other options, are you?'

Turning to face Joe, Colin puts the torch between his teeth and stands in front of his friend. He scratches at the floor with his right foot, flaps his arms up and down and clucks. He takes one pace back – scratches, flaps, clucks – and then another pace and then another, daring Joe – and himself – to enter the room.

Joe follows. He has been called chicken. He is powerless to do anything else.

Colin swings torchlight around the chamber, tries to hold his breath and speak at the same time. 'Shit,' he says, words muffled by closed lips.

Lit up, the figure of a man. A man crucified on a wooden cross. Upside down on a wooden cross.

Only he isn't really a man: he's an anatomical sketch of what's inside a man – more bone than flesh.

Colin moves close, shines a light on the figure's face.

Nothing.

And then dried parchment skin seems to ripple and the man groans.

Simultaneously, Colin's heart attempts to leave his chest, only to clash with the contents of his stomach as they rise to fill his gullet.

Joe still hovers on the perimeter, disinclined to engage with Colin's terror. A terror that freezes Colin to the spot, unable or unwilling to flee, even though all his animal and street instincts are screaming: 'Get the fuck out, shit-for-brains.'

Thoughts clash, collide, fragment, reform. The groan was obviously a movement of air, something caused by the door being opened after so long but how long was *so long*? How long had this poor fuck been hanging like this? And who was he? Who had he been? And what had he done?

There's a whisper in his ear – a flutter of words soused in unconsecrated earth – and Colin moves closer.

The corpse mewls again.

Colin jumps back. 'Man!'

Joe calls across from the furthest corner. 'What? What is it?'

'He's alive,' Colin says, unable to look away.

'What should we do?'

'Don't know.'

The rotten smell is stronger now. Lips move. Colin leans in. 'What's that?'

Eyes open. Less plea, more command.

'OK,' Colin says. Reaching down, he pulls at a large iron nail piercing the man's left wrist, pinning it to the cross's armature.

'Col? What you doing, Col? What you doing?'

'Helping the man.'

'Why?'

'He told me to.'

Colin tugs the nail free. The man stretches out his arm, flexes his fingers.

Colin notices that the man doesn't have fingernails, he has talons but it doesn't matter.

Nothing matters, not anymore.

The man moves his lips, his words indistinct, lost.

Colin leans in still closer. 'What's that?'

The man's arm describes an arc through the air with Colin's throat at its apogee. The talons make an incision which starts under Colin's right ear, slicing away epidermis and dermis before severing his right sterno-cleido mastoid muscle.

The hand carries on across and inside Colin's throat, following the line of his chin through his external and internal carotid arteries, his jugular vein, his oesophagus – where it separates larynx from trachea and rips through the mucous membranes of his vocal folds, silencing his screams – before severing the second sterno-cleido mastoid muscle and exiting just proud of his left ear.

As Colin bleeds out and the man tongues clean his fingers, Joe turns and runs into the outer chamber, starts scrabbling at the bricked-up door.

Colin's attacker frees his other hand.

Next, he folds his chest up and over his legs and looses his ankles from the heavy iron collar which holds them against the wooden upright.

And then he's gone.

In a blink, he vanishes.

Only to reappear three feet behind Joe.

Two feet behind Joe.

One foot behind Joe.

Joe turns.

High above, Charlie-Boy takes the screams and the silence which follows to be a prompt – he isn't going to get another opportunity like now. Whatever it takes, however much pain, he should get going. Get going from here, get going straight, get going somewhere no one knows him.

Just plain get going

Shock and awe.

The creature stands in a state of shock and awe.

Familiar sensations flooded through him as he crawled up the wall – his body working instinctively, muscles and ligaments stretching and cracking, fingers and talons digging, prying, gripping – but before that, even as he felt his body coming back to what he knew as life, there is something else.

Something alien, unknowable.

At first, it's a taste in his mouth.

This is followed by a numbness in his tongue – a feeling which rapidly spreads through his jaw and into his face.

And then there's the light, a single pinprick of light.

The pinprick expands, bringing sights, sounds, sensations

Screeching alarms bellow like banshees through brutal stone jungles, while feral children clamber across landscapes of unrecognisable harshness. All to a dreadful, hellish music composed entirely of rhythm and no discernible melody.

From a distance, a moment of realisation: it's the blood – there is some strange, befuddling chemical concoction in the blood. He felt something similar the night they'd ensnared him, entombed him, prayed never to see him again. But here he is and where are they? Long gone no doubt, all rendered nothing more than dust and smut in the cracks and folds of Digbeth's crenulated history.

And now here he is, standing out in the open, his feet wet.

Wet?

He looks down.

Up to his ankles in liquid clay, the ground rises to swallow him.

He glances around and his vision stutters. It's as if he's in a bioscope show with a faulty lantern, every image lingering on the screen, a beat after it should have vanished.

A steam train flickers and fades across a white wall.

No, that is definitely real: his first ever visit to The Electric Theatre – that isn't now, that was in the past.

He looks down again: the earth is up to his waist. He struggles, its grip tightens and he's gone.

Head under clay, he tastes sandstone as Victorian Birmingham unspools before his eyes.

The pigs marshalled through Digbeth to the Bull Ring. The squeal of slaughter and the smell of iron.

Of blood.

The clang of metal on metal.

Irish, Italian, Welsh, Scots, Jews – they all come to Birmingham, to Digbeth, to do business, to trade, to live, to die.

At night, the music halls are filled with cheap music designed to fill even cheaper lives. And life is cheap. Especially at night.

Especially when it screams.

And then, unbelievably, silence.

The barking hokey pokey men have disappeared.

The beggars closed their lips.

The High Church aristocracy retreated to their country haunts.

The plague is in decline but the silence shocks him more than the corpses. Of course it does: death is part of his existence but silence?

Digbeth is never, ever silent. It's a living, bellowing beast that tolerates him for the obedience he creates – obedience underwritten by fear.

Now he's surrounded by dwellings marked with a red cross, places that even he knows best to avoid. They appal him so, the fresh dead, with their clawed hands beseeching a forgiveness they can never receive and their slack-jaws gaping at the world, as if in wonder.

Later – earlier – the plague arrives in a box of clothes from London, the courier staying in Digbeth's north side, at the White Hart Inn on the corner of Allison Street and Park Street.

He blinks and years before the fleas, sulphur burns the air and sparks fly from each and every front room.

And each and every in-breath feels like a breath drawn in hell.

There's the stench of piss, too, as freshly hewn hide is stewed into leather.

He sinks further.

The air clears. He passes tight plots of land marked up and allocated to broken-backed farming families.

Deeper still, he touches shattered erotic pottery, the shrapnel of a retreating empire.

And now the Romans have yet to arrive but travellers from the East are here, with their binding spells and incantations, drawing a line of defence around the seven hills that surround their settlement, the slender rivers, the plentiful springs.

Spells and incantations designed to keep him at bay.

But whose land is it?

Didn't these people themselves come sailing from somewhere else? Aren't they the scrawny remnants of a fallen satrapy? And why aren't they content to inhabit the day, leaving the night to its own?

To him.

And then they've gone, these interlopers, back to their risen city-state, waiting for the horse hewn from timber that will deliver their inescapable demise.

Earlier still, running through a moonlit forest, the floor springing at his feet, the scent of life in his nostrils, he hears human sounds, he sees human shapes.

Closer, closer, closer, until his victim lies beneath him, little more than child, little more than beast. A hand opens and an axe tumbles free, sliding down the bank towards the river. The body trembles as it dies. This human male had no hopes, no dreams, no aspirations beyond warmth, shelter and scavenged food.

It had no life and now it has no life.

He has no guilt.

Whatever path home his victim had chosen, it chose wrong. He is a predator: this dead thing and its kind are and always will be his prey.

From cave to pavement, always the prey.

Earlier still, he crouches on his ankles under a full moon, giving thanks to the full-bodied bright goddess that dominates his life. In almost his first moment of cognition, he realises it is the rare but successful animal which hunts during darkness and this rarity gives him advantage.

His distant cousins live by day and struggle, he lives in the shadows and prospers. In time, he will become the shadows.

Become their shadow.

And then a thought: perhaps this time is his time and that the cellar is the illusion, a foretelling of things to come.

As he visualises the cellar, he begins to rise, swimming upwards through the earth. Dimly, he realises that the clay and sandstone aren't real, just some mesmerism brought on by whatever narcotic runs through his blood. But even as he returns to his corporeal present, he can smell primeval forest mist commingled with the urban smog of industrialisation. He can sense the thrum of a thousand generations as they tell horrific tales around open hearths of peat and gas, coal and electricity. He can hear wolves howl, hear them scratching at the door. They want to come in but they don't belong here: they died long ago and are simply memories.

Somebody else's memories.

Or maybe these memories are his.

Maybe these memories are his only real memories.

He'd forgotten quite how difficult it could be to differentiate himself from all the other lives that occasionally rekindle inside his head.

Rekindle and demand attention but never like tonight.

Never with such vim, vigour, vitriol.

Staring up at the sky for the first time in an age, he feels belittled, lost, torn from everything he understands. For as long as he can remember, he's thrived in the gloom of peoples' fear — his presence, his vitality, given flesh by the contrast between the human capacity for hope and the dread that enrobes the soul just before dawn.

Only now the world clock is stuck at four in the morning and humanity has become anaesthetised by a new pitch of existence. Somehow this species' psyche has altered beyond recognition and what had once sent them scurrying for cover, reduced them to animals hiding in hollows, begging for salvation, is gone.

He watches as a damaged figure drags itself across a barren landscape of broken brickwork and rain-filled pits. It trails the smell of fresh blood but all he feels is an overwhelming sense of indifference.

Detachment.

Ennui.

He knows that this world is no longer his.

He knows that he is out of time and out of place.

And in this knowledge, he feels lost.

And in this moment, he feels redundant.

And then he laughs, because no matter how bad mankind has always considered him, mankind is now so much worse.

He turns to the east, the glazed, snaggle-toothed horizon of new Digbeth already tinted the colour of broiled tomato. Closing his eyes, he raises his face, waiting for the warmth of the early morning sun to touch his skin.

Digbeth Burns

MATHEW GOSTELOW

She is a spring, a surging overflow of fiery water. She is Dyke Path and Duck Bath. A factory font of instant inspiration. She lives on the east side where the blazing light is born, where we learn the gift of seeing. When creative wells run dry, I make pilgrimage to draw her power, to forge myself anew within her furnace, to walk her shadowed arches, lose myself in echo-stepping rabbit-holes and alleyways. I drink her atmosphere through open pores. By rites invoke her vision, art, and craft.

The first guardian, Alfie Mo, looms high, thirty feet or more above my head. Overseer, gigantic, skinny-slim. He sports a hipster 'tache and slacker jeans, and shares with me his visionary dreams, clear from unclouded altitude. His namesake's factory repurposed now, producing golden flows of sweet inspiration. I photosynthesise his novel ways of seeing, the glow that's pouring viscous through his doors.

Nearby, Jack of the Green sprouts organic, bursting from the brutal brick, all bark and bite and fecund shoots. I gaze upon his leafy face, dwarfed beneath his sap-sprung stems, to learn his gift of life-spark. He shows me how the seed of an idea, so small, innocuous, dense-packed, might rocket into glorious creation. Firework flowers bloom fresh from my mind's rich soil.

Witch familiar, Annatomix fox, she creeps and slinks, brick red across the painted walls. Her green-eyed headlight gaze can teach the fires of alchemy. I swirl into her melting pot of cultures and ideas, where magic burns in coloured dancing flames — vermillion, viridescent, amber-gold. She shares with me enchantments made through new and wild concoctions, ingredients unstable, mixed to fulminate and dazzle with ferocious novelty.

Upon her head the Old Crown rests, a place more old than war or memory. Beamed walls awash with words and ale and song. Spirits haunt her cobwebbed crooked rooms, echoes of folk who seek new ears to hear their creaking dusty tales once more. I tangle in their stories' silken threads until I tumble free to spin them out anew.

Her walls are tattooed rainbow spraycan hues, scrawling street art symbols, a sprawling hypersigil to inspire transformation, vivid lucid dreams displayed in concrete galleries. Pieces, burners, tags, and bombs explode energetic on her limbs. I lose myself within her streets until her blessing tints me with new colour. I lean upon her walls and soak the pigment of ideas. I run among her tunnels to find magic in the dark. For Digbeth burns with bright creation's spark.

About the editors

GARRIE FLETCHER

Garrie Fletcher writes short stories, scripts, and novels. He runs creative writing workshops in prisons, mental health settings, schools, museums and for Writing West Midlands. He has been published by Unthank Books, Blackheath Books, *3:AM Magazine*, Dostoyevsky Wannabe, MIR Online and many others, including Mantle Lane Press who have put out two books, *Night Swimming* and *Submerged*, as well as his short story *Electricity* in their *Songs of the Elephant Man* anthology.
Blog: fletchski.com
Twitter: @fletchski

PETER HAYNES

Peter Haynes' short fiction has been published widely online and in print. His debut novel *The Willow By Your Side* was published in 2018.
Twitter: @PHaynesWriter

NIGEL PROCTOR

Nigel Proctor has been drama student, van driver, waiter, failed rock'n'roll star, copywriter, and film critic. Now into his 4th decade as an award-winning professional filmmaker, he's a decent stills photographer but a somewhat better cook. His debut novel *Fire Damage* is a police procedural set during the Birmingham Blitz, November 1940.
Twitter: @nigelproc
Instagram: @nigelproc

About the authors

RACHEL SAMBROOKS

Rachel Sambrooks is a writer and performer from Birmingham. She has a poetry pamphlet published by Palewell Press, had work broadcast on BBC Radio and is developing her writing on a Developing Your Creative Practice grant with Arts Council England. She produced and hosted *Stand by Your Nan* a podcast about grandmothers and tours the live show. Her poetry has been longlisted for Bridport Prize, the CLiPPA award and she won City of Stories for Merton. She is a member of the Room 204 development scheme with Writing West Midlands.
Website: rachelsambrooks.com
Twitter: @rachsambrooks
Instagram: @rachelsambrooks

KATE MASCARENHAS

Kate Mascarenhas writes fiction. An earlier version of *Berkhead* appeared in *A Spell to Conjure Violets* (2016). Birmingham is also the backdrop for Kate's latest novel, *Hokey Pokey*, a supernatural story set in a 1920s grand hotel.
Website: katemascarenhas.co.uk

JAMILA BARRY

Jamila's grandparents came to Birmingham from Ireland, and she's raised their great-grandchildren here; it's their home. Although they've moved abroad many times, they always end up back in Brum. She loves to share her pride in this bustling, beautiful, grimy, inclusive city. Having written snippets of stories for years, this is her first time being published.

STEPHEN GOODYEAR (1937–2021)

Unfazed by the poverty he was born into, Stephen learned that incredible things can be achieved with confidence and self-belief. Defying the gods, he saw beauty and possibility everywhere, even in the toughest of circumstances. For him, community was everything: look after your neighbours, look after your friends and most certainly look after your family — even if they are a little rough around the edges.

LAURENCE INMAN

Laurence Inman has done many things, most of them not very well. His three children, however, are very successful.

MEAVE HAUGHEY

Meave Haughey is a short story writer based in Birmingham. Recent stories have been published in Comma Press's *The New Abject* and *Forecast: New Writing from Birmingham*, Dostoevsky Wannabe's *Love Bites: Fiction Inspired by Pete Shelley and Buzzcocks* and in *Birmingham*, from the Dostoevsky Wannabe Cities series. *The Reservoir* was included in *The Best of British Short Stories 2021* published by Salt.
Twitter: @writemeave

CHARLIE HILL

Charlie Hill is a writer of fiction and memoir who has been described by Natalie Haynes as 'the chronicler Birmingham needs'. He has spent many years drinking and working in Digbeth.
Website: charliehill.org.uk

KIT DE WAAL

Kit de Waal was born in Birmingham to an Irish mother, who was a childminder and foster carer and a Caribbean father.

She worked for fifteen years in criminal and family law, was a magistrate for several years and sits on adoption panels. She used to advise Social Services on the care of foster children, and has written training manuals on adoption, foster care and judgecraft for members of the judiciary.

Her writing has received numerous awards including the Bridport Flash Fiction Prize 2014 and 2015 and the SI Leeds Literary Reader's Choice Prize 2014 and the Kerry Group Irish Novel of the Year.

My Name Is Leon, her first novel was published in 2016 and shortlisted for the Costa Book Award. She has two children and lives in the West Midlands.

TOM MAGUIRE

Tom Maguire is an aspiring author originally from Great Barr, Birmingham, now based in the city centre. His writing lies somewhere in the tradition of Weird speculative fiction and incorporates influences from his background in Philosophy and Critical Theory. He DJs in his spare time and you can occasionally catch him around Digbeth playing Dub, Jungle and UK Garage.
Instagram: tmdubz1.
Soundcloud: tm_w

KIRSTEN HANDLEY

Kirsten is a daydreamer which lends itself pretty well to writing stories. She moved to Birmingham for University in 2011 and fell in love with the warmth and friendliness of the city. She has featured in a number of Birmingham based anthologies including *City at Night, City of Echoes and Time*. Her short story *Ice* also featured in *FlashFlood 2020*. She attends Birmingham Writers Group as a great way to meet more local writers.

TAYLOR BURNS

Taylor Burns is a graduate of City University's Novels MA programme, for which he received a distinction. He is currently seeking representation and trying to find a home for his first novel, *Travis Barnes (In All His Raging Glory)*. Elsewhere, he has been published at *The Common Breath* and in the American poetry journal, *Rattle*. He lives in Birmingham. Pulls pints sometimes.
Instagram: taylor___burns (with 3 underscores)

MATTHEW GIDLEY

Matthew Gidley is working on a collection of short stories set on the River Rea between 1000BCE and the present day. He lives in Kings Heath. He wishes to thank Valerie Edden for helping Lob find his voice.

KAREN ARNOLD

Karen Arnold is a writer and psychotherapist born in the Black Country and living in Worcestershire.
Twitter: @aroomofonesown_4

JOSH ALLEN

Josh Allen is a contemporary historian, writer, journalist and occasional curator from Birmingham. He produces *Walk Midlands* an online guide to day walks in the English Midlands accessible without a car, for walkers interested in all aspects of the region's people, landscape and history.
Twitter: @aroomofonesown_4

BEN WADDINGTON

Ben Waddingtonis the author of *111 Places in Birmingham That You Shouldn't Miss* and the director of *Still Walking*, a Birmingham-based festival with an annual programme of guided tours and walking events. Cup Song is his first venture into fiction.

ALAN BEARD

Alan Beard is a short story/flash writer with two published collections: *Taking Doreen out of the Sky* (Picador, 1999) and *You Don't Have To Say* (Tindal St Press 2010). He won the Tom Gallon Award for best short story. Stories on BBC Radio and in many magazines and anthologies, including *London Magazine*, *frieze*, *Malahat Review*, and *Best Short Stories* in 1992 and 2011.

CHARLIE ROSE EVANS

Charlie Rose Evans is a Brummie writer and trade union receptionist. She enjoys writing short stories and poetry about family, childhood, and local history.
Instagram: @charlierosewrites

PATRICK BOYDEN

Although he was born in London, from the age of three Patrick lived in north Birmingham. His formative years were in the sixties and seventies, the age when every boy wanted to be in a rock band. He eventually got his wish, playing bass in a band whose main claims to fame were being thrown out of the Barrel Organ in Digbeth and earning more in VAT refunds than in gig fees (there were two accountants in the group). The arrival of punk, plus increasing domesticity, put an end to the band's ambitions. His musical career had an enjoyable reprise in the new century playing pubs, birthdays and weddings in a blues and rock band. Patrick is now retired from proper work and lives in Greece where traditional music is played in 9/4 or 13/4, or so it seems. Strange times.

ZAHIRA P. LATIF

Zahira is a former academic and a British Pakistani Muslim woman from a working-class background. She has had creative non-fiction pieces published in *Porridge*, *the Wilderness House Literary Review*, and *The Preservation Foundation*. Zahira is currently working on her first non-fiction book, a polemical critique of the implications of capitalism on our well-being. She lives with her family in Birmingham, England, United Kingdom.
Twitter: @zplatif

HELEN CROSS

Helen Cross's stories have been published in many magazines and anthologies including most recently the *Manchester Review* and *Popshot* magazine. She is the author of four novels including *My Summer of Love*, which became an award-winning movie. Two of her original screenplays are currently in development with UK film companies and her audio dramas are regularly broadcast on BBC Radio. Her most recent work is the podcast drama series, *English Rose*. Seasons 1 and 2 currently available on BBC Sounds.
Website: helencross.net
linktr.ee/helenxwriter
Twitter: @helenx-writer
Instagram: @helenx-writer

JOEL BLACKLEDGE

Joel Blackledge is a writer and filmmaker born and raised in Birmingham. He has been published by *Unbound, Vittles, Architecture Foundation, Novara Media, [in]Transition*, *Little White Lies*, and BBC Radio.

RICHARD LAKIN

Richard Lakin studied chemistry before working as a police officer, salesman and journalist. He writes short stories, non-fiction and scripts. His work has been published in the *Guardian, Telegraph, Londonist, Structo* and elsewhere.
Blog: richlakin.wordpress.com

ALAN KANE FRASER

Alan Kane Fraser was born in Handsworth, Birmingham in the era when that district was famous for its riots. He has been variously a priest, a housing officer, and a charity CEO, in which capacity he wrote for a number of publications, including the *Guardian*. He is also the author of an award-winning play, *Random Acts of Malice*. His novel, *The Muse of Hope Fall*s will be published in late 2023 by Lightning Books. He still lives in Birmingham, with his wife and a woefully inadequate number of bookshelves.

SARAH SPILSBURY

Sarah Spilsbury is a Smethwick based writer of fiction and drama/actor/tour guide/housing officer and is known by that name on Facebook and Twitter. They are a member of West Bromwich Writers' Group and are in the process of tidying up a novel about a nineteenth century maverick medium/pharmacist /pornographer/showman/suffragist. Other interests include podcasts /local history/rambling/Archers fandom.

MATHEW GOSTELOW

Mathew Gostelow (he/him) is a fledgling writer whose strange tales have been published by *Lucent Dreaming, Janus Literary, Ghastling, Ellipsis, Cutbow*, and others. He was nominated for the Pushcart Prize in 2022 and has won prizes from *Bag of Bones* and *Bear Creek Gazette*.
Twitter: @MatGost

Acknowledgements

PETER: We are grateful to the following people for their help creating the Digbeth Stories collection: Kit de Waal, Jonathan and everyone at Writing West Midlands, Prof. Gregory Ledbetter at BCU, the English departments at Newman College and the University of Birmingham, the team at Centrala in Digbeth for hosting a great kick-off event, Clive and Maria at Voce Books & everyone at the Warehouse Café, Catherine and Claire at The Heath Bookshop, and everyone who spread the word on our behalf. And of course, all those who provided kind testimonials.

GARRIE: Thanks to my incredible family, Juliet, Jude and Amber for supporting and encouraging me in this insane venture, Clive Russell for professional advice and his long-standing friendship, our great writers for submitting and working with us, and to my fellow long-suffering editors for not shooting me when a bullet would've made most sense.

NIGEL: Thanks to Caroline, Rachel and Katy for the many times they were woken by frantic keyboard tapping and the smell of a burnt moca pot, as I learnt to write during those gaps in my day job that were meant to be family holidays. To Kevan Brighting, Jenny Lecoat and Gary Lawson who have never been anything but encouraging. To Jeremy Pattle for his constant friendship as well as his musicianship. And to Garrie and Peter: it's been a complete pleasure, here's to the next one.

And finally, thanks to anyone and everyone who had to put up with our long periods of distraction and absence as we learnt how to ride the bucking bronco that is publishing.